"You need help?"

Oh, no.

Alyssa stared up into Trent's face. "No, I'm fine, actually. I was just..." She tried to pull herself up and out of the jungle gym tunnel, but her cuff was caught.

Before Alyssa could protest, Trent caught her arms and pulled.

"I wasn't really stuck." She nodded her daughter Cory's way. "We were playing a game."

"But you were," Cory protested. "You wescued her, mister."

He smiled. "You can call me Trent."

"And you can call me Cory. And now we can be fwiends."

A group of small children entered the playground from below. Cory turned, hopeful. Alyssa nodded their way. "Yes, go ahead."

Trent moved toward the slide. "It seems there's only one way down. I'll go first."

He slid down, then stood grinning from the ground below. "Your turn."

Was it the thought of her getting caught on the slide that sparked his grin or was he just trying to cajole a laugh out of her?

As he did so long ago...

Books by Ruth Logan Herne

Love Inspired

Winter's End
Waiting Out the Storm
Made to Order Family
*Reunited Hearts

*Men of Allegany County

RUTH LOGAN HERNE

Born into poverty, Ruth puts great stock in one of her favorite Ben Franklinisms: "Having been poor is no shame. Being ashamed of it is." With God-given appreciation for the amazing opportunities abounding in our land, Ruth finds simple gifts in the everyday blessings of smudge-faced small children, bright flowers, fresh baked goods, good friends, family, puppies and higher education. She believes a good woman should never fear dirt, snakes or spiders, all of which like to infest her aged farmhouse, necessitating a good pair of tongs for extracting the snakes, a flat-bottomed shoe for the spiders, and the dirt...

Simply put, she's learned that some things aren't worth fretting about! If you laugh in the face of dust and love to talk about God, men, romance, great shoes and wonderful food, feel free to contact Ruth through her website at www.ruthloganherne.com.

Reunited Hearts
Ruth Logan Herne

Love Inspired

Recycling programs for this product may not exist in your area.

 LOVE INSPIRED BOOKS

ISBN-13: 978-0-373-87666-2

REUNITED HEARTS

Copyright © 2011 by Ruth M. Blodgett

www.LoveInspiredBooks.com

Printed in U.S.A.

Can a mother forget the baby at her breast and have no compassion on the child she has borne? Though she may forget, I will not forget you! See, I have engraved you on the palms of my hands.

—*Isaiah* 49:15, 16

This book is dedicated to my four boys,
Matthew, Seth, Zach and Luke, four delights in my life
whose antics and humor have kept me laughing, which
is about the only thing that spared their lives some days.
Thanks for the constant kudos, the love,
the support and your belief in me. I'm so grateful.

And to Jon, my erstwhile and kindly son-in-law,
a gentle man in all respects. I love you guys.

Acknowledgments

First to Rene, Patty, Colleen, Rita, Andrea, Fran,
Meaghan and Susan, who've steadfastly believed.
To my buddy Kevin, who's read them all
and makes me feel good about myself. You guys rock!
To the Song-Prayers, who've been wonderful supporters,
first readers and have my back in times of trouble.
I love you guys, prayer-warriors all. My day-care moms,
such a great group of women. I love that you
entrust your precious children to *Baby: Survivor.*

To my family, who juggle their schedules to help mine.
I could not ask for more, except maybe more chocolate.
And a maid. A maid would be really nice.
Thanks to Jason Sweeney for his advice on
military contracts and contacts, and to
Lieutenant Colonel Tim Hall from MIT for his advice
on military education and command. Huge.

Thanks to Cher Neidermeyer and Glenn Pierce of the
Ronald McDonald House in Rochester, and a special
thanks to Dr. Vermilion and Bernadette of the Golisano
Children's Hospital at Strong. Thank you for your time
and expertise, helping me get it right. I'm very grateful.

To Dave for sitting next to me in church, jumping in all
over the place and pretending to love sandwiches, dust
and clutter. Your gentle support is a true blessing.

Chapter One

Two words jerked Trent Michaels out of his comfort zone, tunneling him back a dozen years, pre-West Point, pre-deployment, a young man searching for answers. For hope.

"Alyssa. Hello."

Heart pumping from a swift adrenaline punch, Trent stared straight ahead as his high school love leaned down to accept his new boss's hug, looking...

Amazing. Beautiful. Wonderful.

His heart ground to a stop, unwilling to believe what his eyes held true. Dark brown hair, clipped back, framed a face no less beautiful at thirty. Probably more so, the mature features offering a true version of what girlish looks had only hinted. Dark brows arched over hazel eyes, tiny spikes of gold lighting the color from within, her profile as dear and familiar now as it had been twelve years past.

But what was she doing in Jamison, New York?

He'd checked before accepting Helen Walker's offer of military liaison with Walker Electronics. A good soldier always appraised his front line, and Trent had a slew of battlefield commendations testifying to his thoroughness. As of last week, Alyssa had been living in a squirrel's hole-sized town in eastern Montana.

"How's your father, dear? The surgery went well, I hear?"

Lyssa nodded, her expression warm, a small smile curving

soft, sweet lips he remembered like it was yesterday. "Yes, thank you, although he's already chomping at the bit. My mother has her hands full."

Helen clucked womanly empathy. "I'll bet she does, but at least you were able to come back." She squeezed Lyssa's hand in a silent message, her look sympathetic. "That's a big help right there."

"I hope so." Lyssa straightened, her gaze traveling the table full of men with a polite smile of welcome, right until she came to him.

She stopped.

Stared.

So did he.

One hand came to her throat in a convulsive movement. She didn't look happy to see him. Shocked, yes. Surprised, absolutely.

And scared. No, wait. Make that petrified.

Trent had become an expert in tactical assessment during his long stint in the military, but his current appraisal made little sense.

A second ticked by. Then two. And suddenly a voice interrupted the moment, a familiar voice, yet not one he'd heard in a long time. Twenty years, give or take, because it was *his* voice, his voice as a child, the speaker obscured by a curved oak support draped in grape vine and clear twinkle lights.

"Excuse me, Mom?"

Lyssa turned, her face ashen. Her gaze darted from Trent to the silhouetted boy, her expression mouse-on-the-glue-board trapped. Her lips moved, but nothing came out.

The boy moved closer.

Trent saw *his* face, *his* hair, *his* shoulders as they'd been twenty years before, the boy's stance, his smile, his look of question totally Trent Michaels.

He froze, tight and taut, his head unwilling to digest what his gaze held true.

"Jim says I'm all set in the kitchen. Can I go back to Grandma's now? Practice my throws?"

She nodded, still silent, the beat of her heart evident beneath a ribbed knit top, her breathing tight and forced.

"Yes. I'll see you later."

The boy escaped through the nearest exit. Once outside, he ran for the hillside, barreling downward, his movements lithe with natural athleticism.

Trent had no idea when he'd stood, but he was standing now, his brain processing the scene.

And disbelieving.

Alyssa swiped hands against her pants, then headed for the office, the only private spot in the place, knowing he'd follow. Knowing he had no choice.

He followed her into the room, closed the door with a decided click, then braced himself against the door, shoulders back, chest out, hoping his posture intimidated her and not caring if it did because he was fairly certain that if his stance didn't worry her, the unveiled anger in his voice would. "Alyssa, what have you done?"

She couldn't breathe. Couldn't think. Couldn't possibly reason how this happened after all those years of being so careful and cautious, tucked away in an obscure corner of brushland Montana.

And now...

Alyssa tried to draw a breath, but the look on Trent's face, the pain vying with anger, the hurt...

What she'd seen as good and sacrificial twelve years before seemed completely selfish now.

Dear God, please. Please.

So now you pray, an inner voice scoffed. *You might have wanted to think of that somewhere along the way, missy. A little late at this point, don't you think?*

Shame cut deeper.

Trent's gaze knifed through her, his locked-arm position forbidding. When she stayed silent he strode forward, stopping just short of contact. "Why?"

She shrugged, fighting for words, her closed throat prohibiting speech.

He grabbed her upper arms, anger trumping the sorrow in his face. "I wasn't good enough, was that it? Did Daddy decide I wasn't worthy enough to know I had a son? So he sent you away to avoid the embarrassment of knowing I fathered his grandchild?"

"No."

"And you let him?" Trent railed on, ignoring her protest. "You let him send you away, carrying our child, our son, and never told me, Lyssa? Never gave me the chance to do the right thing? How could you? Did I mean that little to you?"

Pain coursed his features again. His grip tightened and she braced herself, experience telling her what came next, feeling the power and strength magnified by the anger and hurt in his face, his eyes.

Oh, his eyes.

Wet with unshed tears, a glimpse of the boy she'd known and loved shone through, the boy who never cried, never gave up, his stoicism on and off the football field renowned. To see what she'd done to him, what she'd brought him to—

Dear God, please…

Please…

He released his hold, stepping back, his face contorted. "Why?"

The hard edge in his voice straightened her backbone. She drew a breath, squared her shoulders and met his gaze, determined to take her just due. Hadn't she learned that over the years? That life handed out punishments on a regular basis? With the feel of Trent's vise-like grip a fresh memory to join a host of older ones, she raised her chin. "I gave you choices you wouldn't have had otherwise, Trent. And that's all I have to say right now."

* * *

All she had to say?

He stepped forward again.

She cringed, her expression a mix of fear and dread.

Trent stopped cold.

He'd never scared a woman. Ever. The very thought sickened him, but the look on her face, no, scratch that, the look he put on her face, was mortal fear.

He needed time and space to sort this out, to deal with the anger coursing through him, an anger that seemed quite justified under the circumstances.

He turned, put his forehead to the door and breathed deep, realizing that the CEO of Walker Electronics and her team had witnessed the entire spectacle.

The Army had worked to prepare him for surprise attacks, but nothing in their tactical maneuvers readied him for this.

A boy.

A son.

Hidden. Furtive. Kept secret.

Thoughts of his childhood coursed through him, of how hard he worked to become who he was because of who he'd been, the cast-out four-year-old thrown away by vagrant parents passing by on I-86, saved by a pair of hunters who rescued him on a cold, windy, sleet-filled afternoon, hypothermic, hungry and dazed.

A host of emotions wrestled for his heart, his soul. Breathing deep, he opened the door without a backward glance or another word. He headed for the exit looking neither left nor right.

Helen Walker might rethink her offer, and with good reason. Most CEOs deplored scandal and he couldn't blame her. He wasn't big on drama himself, and small-town drama to boot? Magnified by a power of ten, minimum.

But there was no way he could face that table of well-dressed executives right now, not with any semblance of self-control. Better he go, get hold of himself, deal with the new hand just given to him in the game of life.

He was a father. Had been one for some time, it seemed.

A boy. His boy. He pinched the bridge of his nose as realization spiked deeper.

Their boy.

Trent shook his head, gripped the nape of his neck to thwart the crushing headache, then climbed into his car, a different man than the one who had arrived short minutes before.

Very different.

Chapter Two

As mundane tasks vied for Alyssa's attention, her thoughts kept slipping to Trent, stymieing her productivity. By ten o'clock she had no idea how she made it through the night.

What was he doing? Thinking? Was he hunting up a lawyer, wanting what had been denied him for so long? A chance to know his son, the child who grew to look more like him every day?

Fear dogged her steps. She avoided Helen Walker's table by staying holed up in the office until Helen's group left. What must they think of her? Of him? Of Jaden?

Regret spasmed her midsection. Her gut had clenched tight upon seeing Trent and hadn't relaxed yet.

Dear God... Dear God...

The lament sounded lame, even to her. She'd wandered away from faith a long time ago and had much to regret in the ensuing years. No way, no how was God breathlessly waiting for her wake-up call. And now that it had come...

"Lyssa." Cat Morrow touched her arm. The concern in the older waitress's voice mirrored her expression. "He didn't know?"

Lyssa leaned her head back, eyed the pressed tin ceiling tiles, bit her lip and shook her head, one tear snaking its way along her cheek. "No. You did?"

Cat sent her a look of disbelief. "Oh, honey, it only takes one look for anyone who knew Trent as a boy. He's the spitting image of his father. Why didn't you tell him?" Cat pulled her into a hug, her embrace unleashing the floodgates Alyssa held in check all night. "Anyone who was around you two knew what was going on. It was written all over your faces. There, there…" Cat crooned, patting her back, much as Alyssa would have done to Cory, her three-year-old daughter. "It's all right."

Alyssa pulled back, grabbed a handful of tissues from the box alongside the register, blew her nose and shook her head. "It's not. I know that. And I know it never will be."

"That's not true—" Cat protested, but Alyssa knew better.

"Trent's an upright guy. Always was. Always will be. He'll never understand what I did."

Cat tipped her head, puzzled. "I'm having a hard time myself," she admitted.

"He couldn't have accepted the appointment to West Point if he knew, not with their rules." Alyssa met Cat's gaze and drew a deep breath, half remorse, half resignation. "Cadets can't be married or responsible for a child. And if Trent knew, he'd have insisted on marrying me, taking responsibility for us." Visions of Trent's hopeful excitement, the goals of a little boy lost finally attainable, danced in her brain as she remembered his joy at receiving the invitation to attend the esteemed military academy. "I couldn't let him do that."

"It was his job to do that," Cat reminded her. "As the father, he had a duty to his child, his son. And for a guy like Trent, whose parents didn't want him, fatherhood's got to be a pretty big deal. He's not like other guys."

Alyssa had discovered that firsthand in Montana. Thoughts of Vaughn Maxwell's temper taught her that all men weren't created equal. And she was grateful to have kept Vaughn's inner nature from Jaden during the short years they were together. Why hadn't she seen through Vaughn's facade sooner? What was she thinking? If she'd been honest with herself, she could have left before the unthinkable happened. But she'd stayed, leaving no one but herself to blame for the consequences.

Shame coursed through her again. "I don't know how to make this right."

Cat's look said that wasn't possible.

Alyssa turned and stared out the window. "What will I tell Jaden?"

"The truth?"

"How?" She faced Cat again and lifted her shoulders. "He'll never trust me again."

"Never's a long time," Cat advised. She shouldered her bag and arched a brow. "The truth shall set you free," she paraphrased. "John's gospel. Smart dude. He was pretty tight with Christ, remember?"

Alyssa couldn't meet her eye. It had been easy to fall away from faith, from God in Montana. Aunt Gee was a free spirit who lived for the moment, and she'd taken Alyssa in when she needed a home. Alyssa had followed suit, for a while at least.

Shame knifed again.

Sure, she'd straightened up after a couple of years. And Gee had actually matured as well, but nothing made up for the choices Alyssa made those first years away. Foolish. Sinful. Self-indulgent.

God? You there? Can we talk?

Cat reached out and gave her a brisk hug, a hug that said she'd somehow find a way. "I'm off tomorrow, but back on Wednesday. I'll see you then, all right?"

Alyssa nodded.

"And if you need me, need a shoulder, need a pal, need more tissues…" Cat's gaze encompassed the dwindling supply on the counter alongside them "…give me a shout. I'm not far away."

"Thanks, Cat."

The older woman shrugged and nodded, knowing. "You're welcome, kid. And pray. Nothing's so bad that God doesn't want us. Hear us. Care for us."

"Right."

Alyssa wasn't about to buy into that line of reasoning, not when she knew better. No one had pushed her to foolish relationships when she'd left. She'd managed that one on her own. And yes, she'd turned it around, had changed things before she met Vaughn, and then…

And then married a guy who hid his angry side until the chips were down and whiskey took the place of sweet tea on the side porch.

She should have seen it coming. There were signs.

She'd ignored them.

Foolish, foolish girl.

And now?

Cat said she should pray. Cat didn't know, didn't understand that there were some things that were unforgivable. Even by God.

Trent went round the whole thing in his head, trudging the sidewalks deep into the night, and still came up with nothing.

He'd loved her. He thought she'd loved him. When she broke things off and headed out west for college, he'd been devastated but man enough to realize he'd broken trust with her by giving in to temptation. Even at eighteen, he was supposed to be the God-sworn guardian, the protector.

He'd failed miserably, then lost the girl besides. His fault, he knew, for not respecting her enough to wait. But obviously he wasn't the only one lacking honor. The thought of the boy rocked Trent back on his heels.

That Alyssa could do such a thing angered him enough to keep him walking the streets, until he was tired enough to fall into the motel room bed hours later, the pain in his head no match for the one in his heart.

A sharp knock woke Trent with a start the next morning.

At least he thought it was morning. He'd drawn the heavy curtains when he'd finally crashed, shrouding the room from light. Noise. People. Life.

Obviously life found him. Housekeeping, maybe?

"Go away. Do not disturb. Clean tomorrow." He growled the words into his pillow, his temples reverberating like a drill unit on parade: Left. Left. Left, right, left.

"Trent? It's Helen. May I come in?"

Helen?

What was his boss doing here on a Tuesday morning? A frightfully early Tuesday morning?

To fire him.

Of course. Totally understandable. Scandal equates loss of job.

Trent sighed, stood, tossed a pillow back to the top of the bed, ran a hand through his hair and pulled open the door. "I'll save you the trouble and the embarrassment of firing me and verbally refuse the offer of employment you extended yesterday, okay?"

Intense morning sun blinded him, the sharp angle piercing the V-angled crack. Helen stepped in, gave him a once-over, tsk-tsked, pulled out the desk chair and sat down. "I never saw you as a quitter, Trent."

"Beats getting axed."

Did a tiny smile soften her gaze? No. Had to be a quirk of the sun. Trent hesitated, unsure of what to do next.

"You've had better days."

Talk about an understatement. "Yeah."

He shut the door, drew open the curtains and let sunlight soften the room. He drew a breath, waved to his slept-in clothes and offered an apology. "I know I look awful…"

She nodded.

"And that scene at The Edge was at best disconcerting."

"Agreed."

"And it's understandable that you don't want or need an executive who comes with scandal preattached."

"And there's where we differ."

"Huh?" Part of Trent's bemused brain kicked into gear, reminding him that former army captains and executives don't say "huh." He cleared his throat, sat on the lower edge of the bed, leaned forward and asked, "Excuse me? I don't understand."

Helen regarded him with something akin to affection. "Trent, I watched you grow up."

"You and everybody else in town."

"True enough. You were an anomaly, a boy set apart by circumstance, but it wasn't your situation that drew attention."

"No?" Trent scowled. "Could've fooled me." Heaven knows he felt like a circus monkey more than once, his tragic family situation touted in local media.

"It was how you handled those conditions," Helen went on. "The grace under pressure, the time you put in studying, learning, practicing, working. We marveled at you and there was many a prayer offered in thanksgiving that we found you in time. That you survived."

Unlike Clay, his little brother, a good little fellow who drowned when he stumbled into a water-filled ditch three counties east. Why couldn't their parents have dumped them together? Then, at least, Clay might have stood a chance. The hollow spot dwelling just beneath Trent's breastbone nudged an arrow of pain.

"So now, you're under pressure again." Helen rose and shrugged. "And I have no doubts that you'll handle it just fine. In fact, this new twist compels you to stay here, help my company compete successfully for those military contracts. You've got a whole new reason to be in Jamison as of yesterday."

He stared at her. "You still want me?"

She held up her wrist, the unadorned watch a quiet message. "I expect you to be setting up your office in an hour. And I'm hoping you brought another suit."

Several, in fact. "Yes."

"Then I suggest a shower, shave, coffee and ibuprofen for that headache you're trying to hide."

A hint of warmth stole over him. "I'm not a big pill popper. I don't have any."

Helen opened her purse, withdrew a small bottle and shook

two tablets into her hand. "They're generic, but they do the trick."

Trent clenched his fist around the pills. "You're sure?"

"Absolutely. Clock's ticking."

It was. Trent gave a brisk nod to the door and headed for the bathroom to get cleaned up. "I'll see you at nine."

Once again a hint of a smile softened her firm jaw. This time he was certain. She headed out, her footfall firm against the utilitarian carpet. "Good."

As her footsteps faded along the concrete walk, Trent caught a glimpse of himself in the mirror.

Bad. Really bad. With morning breath, besides.

And yet Helen still wanted him. Saw promise in his ideas, his work ethic. Last night's startling revelation put his other ethics into question, but she was willing to give him a shot. See if he could help the struggling local economy by procuring defense contracts. Bigger and better military contracts meant more jobs. Heightened production. A trickle-down effect that would help across the board.

Determined, he intended to do just that. She'd bought him time. Time to get to know his son.

His son.

He growled, realizing he didn't even know the boy's name. But he would, he promised himself as he went through his morning ablutions. He'd been raised without a mother or father to call his own, a public spectacle.

His son would have a father who loved him. Cherished him. He knew he couldn't make up for the years lost. He recognized that. But he could do his best to be a good, strong God-fearing father for the years to come. And Trent had every intention of doing just that.

Chapter Three

"Jaden Michael Langley, what are you doing out there with no coat? Your mother will skin you alive if she sees that," Susan Langley scolded from her back door. "Grab a jacket and put a hat on, for pity's sake. At least until the thermometer hits fifty."

"Grandma, I'm fine," he insisted. "Too many layers mess up my throw."

"And if you catch a cold like your little sister, it messes up my schedule and your grandfather's recovery," Susan retorted in a tone that meant business. "Jacket. Now."

Huffing with impatience, Jaden dipped his chin in silent agreement, accepted the jacket she suspended from two fingers, tugged it into place without zipping and raced right back to the old shed where circled numbers marked spots for intended receivers.

"You got him to put a coat on?" Alyssa came down the back stairs, sent her mother a look of appreciation as she overheard the exchange and inclined her head toward the sloping backyard. "I'm amazed."

Susan toyed with her coffee mug, her gaze outward, eyes thoughtful. "He doesn't know me well enough to know I won't go ballistic if he stands his ground. And Jaden's eager to please, he likes making people happy. He's got a lot of his father in him, Lyssa."

"That's for sure."

Her tone drew her mother's attention. Susan turned, questioning. Seeing Alyssa's face, she stepped forward, concern deepening her features. "What's happened?"

Alyssa's heart clenched, the knot of anger and fear tightening. "Trent saw him."

"What?" Susan's face paled. She set her mug down hard, sloshing coffee onto the familiar oak surface, disbelief drawing her brow. "How?"

Alyssa hesitated, grimaced and sighed. "He came into the restaurant last night. With Helen Walker and a bunch of her executives." She shook her head, wishing she'd never approached the table, wishing she could reverse time for those short seconds, wishing…

"Alyssa." Susan braced her hands on Alyssa's shoulders. Her fingers shook, reminding Alyssa she wasn't in this alone. "He saw Jaden?"

Alyssa sent up a silent prayer, a plea, hoping and praying she'd wake up and this would all be a bad dream.

No.

"Do you think he—"

"He knows."

"No."

"Oh, yes." Alyssa walked to the window, tipped the curtain aside with one finger and studied her son, a beautiful boy who grew to look more like his father with each passing day.

A father she'd cheated out of his son.

Trent's words swept through her, the anger and recrimination emanating from him as he faced her in the small, cluttered office. So different from the boy she'd known, the look of hope and promise he wore when he'd received his congressional appointment, knowing he had a chance to do something, be someone, change the world.

She felt sacrificial then.

She felt traitorous now.

"You talked to him?"

"Yes." She leaned her forehead against the cool spring glass, then sighed, sniffed, and shook her head, watching Jaden loft the ball from various angles. The boy's pinpoint accuracy went beyond his years, reflecting his natural ability to weave a pattern and pick a receiver. Of course his height helped, a combined parental gift. Trent's height had made Alyssa feel less freakish in high school. At five foot nine she'd towered over half the boys until growth spurts pushed them to equal or surpass her.

Susan stepped closer and tucked an arm around her shoulders, the show of support inspiring more tears. "You talked with Trent?"

"He talked. I cringed."

"Cringed?" The leap in her mother's voice made Alyssa regret her choice of words. "Did he touch you?"

"No. Yes. I—"

"It's either yes or no." Grim-faced, Susan studied Alyssa, her voice defensive and sharp. "Did Trent Michaels lay a hand on you?"

"Trent Michaels?" Gary Langley's voice cut in, surprise and disparagement weighting his tone. "You saw him? Here?"

"At The Edge last night," Susan confirmed, shifting her look to Alyssa's dad as he labored his way into the kitchen. Discomfort ruddied Gary's features and accelerated his breathing, his post-op condition aggravated by forty extra pounds. Susan shook her head, scolding. "But don't go getting yourself all worked up. You're just out of surgery and need to rest."

Alyssa's internal guilt-o-meter cranked into high gear. She'd already disappointed her father in every way, shape and form. She had no desire to add another heart attack to the list. "Dad, sit down."

"I'm fine," he snapped, waving off their hands. "The doc said I need to walk, need to move around. Stop fussing. So…" He turned his attention back to Alyssa, his gaze taut, his color high. "He's back?"

Forget turning the clock back minutes or hours. Right now Alyssa wished she could spiral the hands back to her senior year, erase Trent Michaels from the picture once and for all, and see what her life would have been like if she hadn't fallen head over heels in love at seventeen. She sighed. "Working for Walker Electronics it seems."

"And he knows about Jaden," added Susan.

Her father scowled, eyes narrowed. "Good. High time he started paying his share."

"Trent would have helped all along. You know that, Dad."

"I know he didn't." Gary lowered himself into a chair, his face a study of pain until he'd settled into position. The chair support allowed him to breathe easier. "Now's as good a time as any to prove he would."

A typical Gary response.

True to form, her father jumped to what had always been the number-one priority in his life.

Money.

"Gary." Susan sat in a chair opposite him and surprised Alyssa with her next words. "You can't blame a man for not taking care of something he didn't know existed. Trent wasn't a bad kid at all. I expect he's turned into a good man."

"Right. A guy who slept with the boss's daughter and got her pregnant. I have a hard time finding the good in that."

"Really?" Susan's arched-brow look deepened his scowl. "Shall we discuss our courtship in front of our daughter?"

Please don't. Alyssa hid a cringe at the thought of her parents being teenagers in love. Some things a girl just didn't need to know.

Gary's frown deepened. "Of course not."

"Then I suggest a little humility," Susan told him. She lowered her chin but held his gaze. "There are a multitude of tender hearts in this house right now, Gary. Not just yours."

Susan's reference to the kids softened Gary's features as she rose to get him a cup of coffee. "Does Jaden know?"

Alyssa shook her head. "No. And he's not going to either. Not till he's ready."

"The size of Jamison?" Gary's expression underscored the unlikelihood of that. Worse, he was right.

"I'll talk to Trent," Alyssa continued. "Explain that Jaden needs time…"

"Or you do."

Alyssa fought the surge of guilt. What would Jaden think of her, to suddenly find out he had a father who had no knowledge of his existence. What kind of liar did that make her? And why did something that seemed noble and necessary twelve years before become such a dark smudge on her soul now?

Trent's face came back to her, that look of betrayal. The shock. The pain. The anger.

But he hadn't tried to hurt her, and that put him one up on Vaughn.

"Mommy?"

Cory's sweet preschool voice squelched the discussion. Alyssa scooped the little girl into her arms, planting kisses along her face and neck.

Cory giggled. "That tickles."

"I know." Alyssa touched her forehead to Cory's. "Your fever's gone."

"Can I still have medicine?"

Cory loved the grape-flavored fever reducer, enough so that Alyssa kept it high and out of sight. "If the fever comes back. Are you hungry?"

"No."

Alyssa tipped her head. "Not at all?"

Cory shrugged. "Maybe for ice cream. 'Cause I'm sick," she added with a solemn nod to her grandmother.

Susan melted on the spot. "Ice cream helps sore throats. I think it's a good choice this morning. But not every morning," she added.

Her attempt to be stern came up short. Cory's smile had a way of negating the firmest intentions. "Thank you, Grammy. I love you. Can I sit with you, Grampa?"

Gary's stoicism couldn't resist the three-year-old's charms either. "Soon," he promised. "But I bet Mommy can pull up a chair and have you sit right next to me, okay?"

"Okay." She beamed at his suggestion, always ready to com-promise, a Pollyanna child seeking good in all things. Thinking of herself and Vaughn, Alyssa had no idea where the sweet, gentle nature sprang from, but Cory's good behavior had been a blessing in an otherwise-tumultuous life.

Alyssa drew a chair alongside Gary's. Her father's size dwarfed Cory, but he grinned at the petite girl and graced Alyssa with a genuine smile for the first time in over a decade. "She's a special little thing."

Alyssa met his smile and matched it. "She is. And smart as a whip."

"She looks like you, Susan."

Susan nodded as she scooped ice cream into a princess-dec-orated bowl. "I think so, too. I look at Cory and I see the face I saw in the mirror when I was a little girl."

Alyssa smiled at the thought. "I wondered. It's clear she doesn't look like me, and I don't see an ounce of Vaughn in her."

"Was he a good man, Alyssa?"

The unexpected question choked her. Her parents had met Vaughn once when they'd traveled west after she'd announced her marriage. They'd stayed at a local motel for three days, got acquainted with Jaden and met Vaughn during his best-behavior stint.

"Alyssa? Was he?"

Oops. Waited too long. Susan Langley had a way of reading between the lines and timing was everything. "Good points and bad points, Mom. Like most."

Her father shrugged acceptance, but her mother's look said too much. But then, she'd never been able to hide things from her mother. That was part of the reason she stayed away so long. Her mother's warmth and strong Christian spirit were a lot to live up to when you know you've messed up repeatedly.

She faked a smile and nodded toward Cory. "And she got your eyes."

Susan's look of appraisal said the discussion wasn't over, not by a long shot, but she let the change of subject slide. "A gift from my mother. And since she got my name as a middle name, I may just start calling her Cory Sue."

Alyssa laughed. "I think that's darling. Sounds like a Cabbage Patch name."

"It does." Susan laid her hand against Cory's forehead, looked comforted by the lack of heat, and jutted her chin toward Jaden. "He's practicing with Coach Russo tonight, right?"

"Yes." Alyssa took the calendar off the wall and noted a few dates in pencil. "Tonight, tomorrow night and then Saturday. Chris said he'd like to get time in with Jaden before the July football camp at Baileview."

Chris Russo was a local businessman who coached football for a travel team and the high school. His strong coaching was a big part of the local teams' success. Chris and his staff knew how to draw the best out of kids.

"Have you signed him up?" Gary's appraising look said more than his words.

"Soon." No way was Alyssa going to confess her complete lack of funds. Her father had put her on the payroll and refused to charge her rent for the garage apartment she'd be using once she finished repainting the walls. She'd found several half gallons of paint in the basement and used those to freshen the kitchen and living room area.

Susan carefully kept her gaze on Cory. "I'll write the check so you can get him registered. The football camp fills up quickly and I'd hate to see Jaden miss this chance."

"But—"

"Your mother's right." Gary opened the folded newspaper, scanned the headlines, muttered something derogatory about politicians and sighed. "You can pay us back later. Or get the money from Trent. He'd probably be happy to shell out for anything to do with football."

"I'm not after Trent's money."

"Well if he's wearing a suit and working for Helen, money

won't be a problem," Gary noted. "And a man pays for his mistakes in this world."

"Jaden isn't a mistake."

"He's a brother," Cory announced, her expression proud, her lilting voice sincere. Jaden had proven to be a wonderful big brother, gentle and protective of Cory since her birth.

Cory's assertion reminded them of her presence. Alyssa nodded her way, ending the discussion. "Yes, he is, honey." Straightening, she switched her gaze to Susan. "Are you okay with her while I finish up the painting out back? I should be able to move in soon."

"Glad to. And I'm doing the evening shift tonight so you can get things done."

"Mom—"

Susan's look said arguing was pointless. Alyssa nodded, reading between the lines. She'd seek Trent out tonight, discern his intentions. Her father's observation had raised a scary but valid point. Trent appeared well-set financially.

He could bankroll an attorney as a means to an end.

Destitute, living on the kindness of her parents, Alyssa couldn't bankroll lunch. And coming off a rough winter with diminished business in their economically challenged county, she knew her parents' funds were thin. A busy summer season would help, but Alyssa had been raised in the restaurant trade and she understood the debit and credits of a successful business. The Edge needed to bring in either more business annually or pump up their summer trade. But how?

And what on earth was she going to do about Trent?

Fear knotted again, mixed with regret. Why hadn't she taken care of this sooner? Come forward and confessed what she'd done? If she'd met with Trent openly and honestly once he'd graduated from the academy, he'd have been upset but might have understood. At least understood better.

She'd been such a coward….

The prayer resurfaced. Dear God… Please… Please.

Lame, Alyssa. And late, besides. Good try, though. She bit her lip, grabbed an old stained sweatshirt that wouldn't be wrecked by daubs of paint, kissed Cory's cheek and headed out the door. "I've got my cell phone."

Susan's look encompassed the short distance from the house to the two-story carriage barn at the end of the drive. "Seriously? If I need you, I'll walk over."

That made Alyssa smile. "Good point." She swept the phone a look as she tucked it into her pocket. "These things get addictive."

"Only if you let them." Susan's wisdom followed her out the door.

Alyssa had missed her mother's gentle, commonsense directives. Her humor, her steadfast belief in right and wrong, good and evil. Somewhere along the way Alyssa had blurred those borders. She'd made mistakes and made excuses.

Was it too late to begin anew? She hoped not.

Did that scare her to death?

Absolutely.

Chapter Four

Trent pounded up O'Rourke's Hill, pushing more than usual, the thick grass beneath his feet God's carpet, nature's bounty.

But no matter how fast or far he ran, thoughts of Alyssa and the boy refused to be laid to rest.

His son. Half-grown. Looking more like him than he'd have thought humanly possible.

His heart clenched, or maybe it was his gut. At this pace it was hard to tell, but as he rounded the curve leading down to the motel, he saw Lyssa standing there, the evening breeze pushing her hair back, away from a face he knew as well as he knew his own.

What a pity that knowledge hadn't gone more than skin deep.

Another clench hit, mid-stride. Stronger. Tighter. This time there was no doubt his heart was involved. He slowed his pace as she watched him approach, using the time to rein in his emotions.

She studied him, eyes narrowed, jaw tight, worry drawing her brow.

He studied her right back, masking his turmoil. The Army had trained him to show nerves of steel, flat-faced, taciturn. He had no problem employing those tactics now. Drawing near, he noticed little things without shifting his gaze.

Her hands clutched a worn purse held by a frayed strap across her shoulder. Her shoes matched the purse's condition, a coat of polish not enough to mask the dull scuffs beneath. She wore thin blue jeans that fit loosely, not as a fashion statement, more like they were the wrong size. Her short-sleeved top wasn't quite enough for the dropping temperatures, especially in the shadowed overhang. Goose pimples dotted her arms from the elbows down. Right now, after an eight-mile run through the hills, the shadowed cement terrace felt real good to him. He stopped just short of her, eyes locked, noting her rise of apprehension as they came face to face.

At the last minute she shifted her gaze, avoiding the intensity, a quick breath telegraphing her uneasiness.

Or guilt.

Or both.

She had good reason to feel both and he was disinclined to lighten the moment. "What do you want?"

She inhaled deeply, then brought her eyes back to his. A fresh round of goose pimples rose on her forearms, a chill coursing her.

He refused to care. He stood firm, feet braced, shoulders back, chest out. "Well?"

She mulled him a moment, her expression unreadable, her eyes pensive. "I need to know what you're going to do."

Trent snorted disgust and started to turn. She put a hand to his arm, her fingers soft, the grip tight. "Trent. Please."

"Don't 'please' me, Lyssa." He swung back, shrugged her hand away and leaned forward. "You ran off twelve years ago carrying my child, then hid my son from me for over a decade. There is no excuse for what you've done." He enunciated the last words slowly, pumping their intensity with pointed deliberation, then ran a hand through his hair and tried to rationalize her choices. But he couldn't. Nothing excused that behavior. Nothing.

"I know."

Her soft voice paused him. His heart clenched again, this

time a combination of feelings and memories waging war for top billing.

He'd loved that voice once. Soft and deep, a little breathless, the raspiness making it stand out. How many times over the years had he turned, hearing a similar voice, his ears drawn to that unique combination of sweet and sensual, memories spiked by the sound of that voice? It was never her.

Now it was, but the anger and disappointment inside him made the old longing a mockery. He'd loved Lyssa, the sweet-faced, gentle girl who always listened, always smiled, always made time for the lost boy within him.

The woman standing behind him might have Lyssa's looks and Lyssa's voice, but the girl he knew would never have done what this one did. And that only meant one thing.

He'd never really known her at all.

He swallowed a sigh, scrubbed a hand to his face and turned back. The cool shade had offered initial respite from his run, but now his sweaty T-shirt chilled him. Or maybe it wasn't the physical conditions making him colder. He'd been a strong-but-gentle young man, a boy who worked hard but made mistakes. He knew that. For a short while after graduating the academy, he'd made a host of them until his conscience smacked him upside the head. He'd tried to own that over the years.

Seeing Alyssa, knowing what one night had done, nipped at the heels of the man he'd become. Older. Wiser. Stronger. Right now that strength felt more like hardness.

God, I have no idea what to say, what to do right now. Anger consumes me, the thought that I gave my heart and soul years ago only to be deceived. My son, my child…

The thought of those missing years bit deeply.

Alyssa was the one person who understood the burden he'd carried, the hole in his heart over Clay's death. She alone knew of the nightmares he had, images of Clay calling for help while Trent tried in vain to reach him. She knew what fatherhood would mean to him. While he loved and appreciated Jamison's investment in him, their pride in his accomplishments, inwardly he longed to be just another normal kid with a mom and a dad.

She'd pushed all that aside and fled with his son. It was an unforgivable act, unbelievable in its audacity. And now she wanted to talk?

"Trent. Please."

Again the hand. The voice.

He shrugged her off and paced away, ignoring the cold bathing his damp skin.

Suddenly he turned, realization pushing him to face her. "What's his name?"

She looked startled, then ashamed. "I'm sorry. I thought you'd know, that you'd have checked things out today."

He arched a brow, waiting.

"Jaden. His name is Jaden. Jaden Michael Langley."

Jaden Michael.

Warmth curled in his belly, somewhere beneath the cold exterior.

"He's like you, Trent. Sensitive. Good. Kind. If we don't handle this with care, we could ruin him."

"If by 'we' you mean 'me', then take a walk, Lyss." Trent shook his head, meeting her gaze, keeping his expression stern. "Despite any guilt-laying trip you might want to put on me, I'm the wronged party here. Now, anyway."

She angled her head, studying him, her appraisal disconcerting. "What would have happened if I told you, Trent? What would you have done?"

"The right thing." He shifted forward, encroaching on her space. "Married you. Supported you. Loved you and him."

His words pained her, he saw that right off, the shadow of sorrow making him wonder what her choices had cost. But he was too angry to delve into that. Didn't know, didn't care.

But you do, the inner voice chided, unbidden.

He shut it down with a quick rebuttal. *Trust me. I don't.*

"And missed the academy?"

"It was a school. Nothing more. Nothing less. There are schools everywhere."

She faced him straight now, chin raised, her gaze steady. "It was your dream, Trent. And you and I both know that cadets can't be married or have a child. I knew you well enough to know you'd never turn your back on your baby."

"And so you chose to keep him from me. Convenient reasoning, Lyss."

A bitter smile twisted her mouth, pained her eyes. "I was wrong, Trent. I see that now. And saying I'm sorry can't fix it."

"You've got that right."

"But what's done is done." She drew herself straighter, taller, meeting him eye to eye. "Right now we need to focus on Jaden. What's best for him."

"What's best for him is a chance to know his father. His real father," Trent ground out, unyielding. "You've cheated me out of eleven years. I refuse to let you get another day."

"Trent." She moved forward, beseeching. "I can't begin to imagine how angry you are…and I realize you have every right to be."

He met her gaze, expressionless, refusing to be drawn into her mollifying tactics. She'd cheated him, she needed to pay. Easy concept.

"But we can't destroy him with this. We have to think first and go slowly. Step by step."

"You're worried what he'll think of you," Trent observed, standing firm. "Honey, that's the least of my worries right now. Best-case scenario? He realizes his mother is a liar and asks to stay with me. At his age judges are willing to consider the child's wishes."

His words hurt her. He saw that and didn't care. No, scratch that, he tried not to care, but her look of pain hit him hard and low.

Because that's how you attacked, his conscience prodded. *And that whole thing about judges? Not very Solomonesque. Try*

Kings, chapter three, verse one. Solomon offered to divide the child to appease the quarreling women. The true mother stood back, refusing her rights to save the child's life. You might want to rethink your options.

He didn't want to.

But the inner voice cast doubt on his absolutism. He stared into space, seconds ticking like minutes, until he finally shifted his gaze back to hers. "What's he doing right now?"

She hesitated. "Practicing football. With Chris Russo."

"He likes it?" Thinking of that, a tiny piece of Trent's heart went out to the boy, a speck of realization that a part of him lived on in someone else. A hint of hope stretched upward.

Lyssa's expression softened, a ghost of the girl coming through the woman. "He loves it."

"Where are they practicing?"

"Behind the middle school. Chris saw his talent right off and asked if he could work with him before the season gets under way."

"I'll work with him."

She looked startled, then frowned. "But—"

"No buts." He leaned in again, refusing to notice the pale points of light in her hazel eyes, how the hint of green to gray sparked amber fire when she laughed. The memory stabbed. He ignored it. "When are they practicing again?"

"Tomorrow, but…"

He shook his head and moved toward his motel room door. "I'll be there. Evening?"

Lyssa stared, gnawed her lip, then nodded. "Yes." She stepped forward, her expression pleading. "You won't tell him, right? Not yet?"

Like he was about to make a promise like that. He'd already been cheated out of a dozen years, give or take. She had no right to set the rules, none at all.

She's his mother, his conscience tweaked once more. *You'd have given anything to have a mother who loved you, remember?*

Oh, he remembered. Too well. A kid doesn't forget when his very own mother equated him with disposable trash, something to cast out, toss by the wayside. Eyeing Lyssa, he saw the difference and wanted to ignore it. Needed to ignore it.

But something in the winsome look of her gaze, a mother pleading for her child, touched him, despite his disdain. He hesitated, worked his jaw and gave a curt nod. "I won't tell him. Yet."

Her look of gratitude evoked guilt within him, and that just made him angry.

Why should *he* feel guilty about anything?

But when she nodded and whispered, "Thank you," it was all he could do to keep from stepping toward her, the voice and expression recapturing times long past, memories of the girl he loved.

Instead he moved backward, eyes narrowed, jaw tight. "Good night."

Chapter Five

"You've looked better." Cat made the observation as she walked into work Wednesday afternoon, her glance skimming Alyssa's face. "Did you catch Cory's cold or have you spent the last forty-eight hours in tears?"

"Most of 'em." Alyssa checked the preset front dining room for table alignment and seating, then turned Cat's way.

"Have they met yet?"

Alyssa hauled in a breath. "Tonight." She tweaked a floral arrangement that didn't need it and sighed. "Trent's going over to the middle school where Chris and Jaden practice. He wants to help."

"Awkward."

"Tell me about it. I told Chris he was coming and he looked at me like I had two heads."

"Chris was a little older, but he knew Trent," Cat reminded her. "Putting two and two together is fairly easy in this case."

"So it would seem."

"And you're worried about what might happen?" Cat mused.

"If by worried you mean scared to death, then yes."

Cat smiled in sympathy and hugged her shoulders. "You can't stop time from moving forward, Lyss. Let go and let God."

"I'm fairly certain God gave up on me somewhere around

Jaden's second birthday." Memories swept her. At the time she considered her options free and unfettered. Now she realized they were just outright selfish. And stupid.

"Honey, we all make mistakes at nineteen. Eventually we get a clue and grow up. You think God holds that against you?"

"Reasonably certain."

"Nonsense." Something in Cat's certainty snared Alyssa's attention. She turned and met her gaze. "Lucky for us, God's better than that. 'As far as the east is from the west I have removed your transgressions from you,'" she quoted. "He's not out to punish us but to embrace us. Sunday school 101." She grabbed Alyssa into a big sister–type hug. "Kiddo, if I thought God turned his back on me, I'd have headed for the hills long ago. He's there. He knows. He loves."

Did he?

Cat's hug felt good. Real good. Alyssa knew enough of the waitress's history to know she'd raised three kids on her own after divorcing an abusive husband, a man who'd used every means in his disposal to keep his wife and kids under his thumb.

But Cat had gotten out. Moved on. With her kids nearly grown and doing well, she'd changed a made-for-TV drama into a success story.

Cat would understand what she'd gone through with Vaughn, how he deliberately robbed her of something precious and pure. For just a moment Alyssa was tempted to tell her, but the phone rang, interrupting them.

Cat sent her a look that offered understanding, then answered the phone. "Good afternoon, you've reached The Edge, Jamison's place for fine dining. How can I help you?"

She raised a brow, nodded toward Alyssa and said, "She's right here, Trent. Just a moment."

Fear gripped Alyssa. Had he changed his mind? Was he calling to let her know he'd decided to tell the boy everything?

Reaching out, Alyssa accepted the phone. "Yes, Trent?"

"I didn't ask what time they were meeting tonight."

"Six-thirty."

"Do you want to pick him up or have me bring him to your parents' place? That's where you're staying, right?" His crisp, clear voice stayed businesslike while hers fought emotion and lost.

"I'll pick him up."

"See you then," he said.

Click.

Dread flooded through her. In two short hours Jaden would come face to face with his father. Would he know right off? Sense the similarities? See the resemblance?

Alyssa had no idea.

Cat read her mind, not that it was all that difficult if the fear claiming her heart was reflected in her face.

"It's not like he's wearing a T-shirt that says, 'Luke, I am your father,'" Cat quoted in a really bad Darth Vader–like voice. "Jaden will see what an eleven-year-old boy should see. A great football player showing him the tricks of the trade. He's looking for a coach. Not a father."

"I hope you're right."

Cat shrugged. "I know I'm right. We see Trent in Jaden because we knew Trent at that age. Jaden will see a cool guy who loves football like he does, a guy who wants to teach him stuff. Give him a leg up. Until someone tips him off, my guess is that's all he'll see."

"Really?" Alyssa wanted to cling to that commonsense hope. Cory's coughing had kept her up half the night, breaking sleep into minute stretches of time and she felt like the fragile threads of her life were at snapping point.

She needed coffee and she needed it now.

"Really," Cat affirmed. She raised her chin as a small group of people walked in the door. "Time to get to work. It's hard to worry when your mind's filled with salad dressing choices and the evening specials."

"Thanks, Cat."

"Don't mention it. And think about what I said. Let go and let God."

Cat's commonsense directive seemed too easy. Her trusted confidante wasn't stymied with layers of guilt on top of a generous serving of self-loathing. On top of that, Alyssa had been raised in a strong, caring family. Sure her dad was tough, but never mean or deliberately hurtful. He was just a dad with high expectations, a goal setter who'd taken a hillside hamburger joint and turned it into one of the area's most sought-out dining spots.

She'd let him down, and instead of learning from her mistakes, she'd repeated them until they cost her more than she cared to admit.

Shame slashed deep.

She believed in God. Always had. But it was hard to imagine the wealth of grace and forgiveness Cat alluded to when Alyssa recognized her role in a host of bad choices.

He's there. He knows. He loves.

Cat's words swirled within her and for just a moment Alyssa wondered if it could really be that sweet, that attainable. Then the image of Trent's face reappeared, lined with anger and disappointment, her betrayal darkening his features. That thought laid to rest any notion of slates swept clean. Penance was part and parcel to life and she obviously hadn't paid up quite yet.

Trent thought it would be simple to walk up to the kid and the coach, reach out a hand and say, "Hey. My name's Trent and I'm here to help."

But to do that he'd have to be able to move his feet forward and for the life of him, Trent stood trapped alongside his car, watching his son dodge and move under Chris Russo's guidance.

The boy's grace was notable. Sure his height added advantage for a junior high player, but more than that Jaden had an inner ability that shone through. Shoulders back, head high, the boy was clearly invested in the coach's advice, nodding agreement all the while.

Trent hesitated.

Should he interrupt this?

He'd been so sure of himself last night, so downright eager to push his presence on the boy, but now he second-guessed himself.

Was he pushing in to punish Lyssa or build rapport with his son?

Jaden.

The name slipped off his tongue like butter on warm bread.

Chris turned, noted him and waved. "Trent. I heard you were stopping by. Come and meet my friend Jaden."

No backing out now. Trent eased forward, keeping his pace even and his face neutral, not an easy task when what he wanted to do was examine everything about the boy, top to bottom. Talk to him, get to know him.

Give him time.

Lyssa's breathy voice came back to him, a woman pleading for her son.

He shoved that aside as he drew near and stuck out his hand. "Jaden, hey. I'm Trent."

The boy nodded amiably. "Good to meet you, sir."

Polite. Straightforward. Nice, good qualities. Lyssa had done well.

"Trent, Jaden and I were just working on the three Ps," Chris offered.

Trent ticked off his fingers, remembering. "Pressure, push, pull."

"Yeah." The boy's smile stabbed through him, because part of Trent wanted the smile to be aimed just at him. Deep down, he hated that he was standing alongside his son, his boy, and the kid had no clue he was shoulder-to-shoulder with his very own father.

But the smile soothed as well, the boy's obvious well-being and good adjustment a huge balm to Trent's tattered soul.

"I'll take center," he offered. Trent exchanged a look with Chris. "I'll snap to Jaden and then you can give him the lowdown on what to do next. What to watch for."

"Good deal," Chris said.

"Hey, guys! Can we work with you?"

Two boys roughly Jaden's age straddled worn bicycles at the field's edge, their looks hopeful. Chris arched an eyebrow toward Trent. "You mind?"

"The more the merrier."

A smile eased the tension he'd noted in Chris's jaw, just enough to tell Trent the other man knew the score, and that raised a question in his mind. Did Chris know because it was that obvious or had Alyssa told him?

The former, Trent decided. He was pretty sure that Alyssa would keep this under wraps as long as she could, but with the striking resemblance between father and son, people would know. That thought was confirmed the first time he saw Jaden lob a spiral that hit his targeted receiver dead-center, the ball's spin textbook-perfect.

"You played before moving here?"

Jaden shrugged. "Not like on a team or anything."

"No?" The boy's reluctant admission raised Trent's ire. "Really?"

"I just practiced a lot."

"Well." Trent mentally chalked the boy's response on his check-this-out-later list and nodded. "It worked. You're solid. Try this, though, when you fade right." Easing back, scanning down field, Trent appeared to be heading right but ended up to the left.

Jaden laughed appreciation for the move. "Do it again. I was too busy watching you to see what your feet were doing."

Trent demonstrated again, noting how Jaden studied his foot moves as if committing them to memory. "That totally jukes the other team."

"Until they figure it out," Trent admitted. "But it's a good move to have in your arsenal."

Jaden nodded. "I'll practice it at home. I like learning new things."

That statement said a lot about the boy's nature. Open. Eager. So much like him. Another knife stabbed Trent, regret twisting within. How he would have loved to guide the boy's first step, his first pass, his first no-training-wheels two-wheeler ride.

But it hadn't happened, and there was no recouping time. Trent's childhood made him understand that better than most.

Three more middle school boys came along and joined the impromptu drills. Studying Jaden's moves, seeing his easy leadership among the other boys, Trent shoved regret aside more than once. Chris left the group with a quick nod of understanding to Trent about an hour later, just minutes before Alyssa pulled to the curb. She stood alongside her car watching, not interrupting Jaden's session, the cool evening breeze making her draw her yellow hoodie tighter.

Trent left the boys to their own devices and trotted her way, pretending not to notice how his approach hiked her anxiety. But her body language spoke volumes. She tightened her stance, shifted her gaze and nervously bit her lip. He couldn't read her full expression because her eyes were shaded by inexpensive sunglasses, the setting sun blinding the east side of the field.

"How did it go?"

"He's amazing."

A tiny smile of agreement softened her clenched mouth. "He is."

"He says he never played formally. Is that right?"

A frown replaced the smile. "That's right."

"Who taught him?"

"He's self-taught mostly. I had a DVD of old Super Bowl games and he'd watch that thing again and again, studying the moves of the players, the teams. And then he'd practice in the backyard, or in his bedroom. He's been running plays since he could walk. So much like you."

Her last words were spoken on a breath of wind, light and soft, wafting away, almost as if she didn't want him to hear them.

But he did.

"Does your husband work with him?"

Her jaw tightened before she shrugged. "He did. Some."

Anger mixed with envy shimmied upward, grabbing Trent

somewhere around his throat. He couldn't imagine having a kid as smart, bright and capable as Jaden and not working with him, not coaching him, not spending every moment he could to help the boy develop skills that opened doors of opportunity. What kind of man shrugged off a kid with Jaden's capabilities? Was it because he was the boy's stepfather?

Trent's defense mechanism clicked into high gear just as Alyssa tried and failed to stifle a yawn. She shook her head. "Sorry."

Something in the way she said that, the way she tried to cover her move, tugged Trent forward. "You okay?"

"Fine."

She wasn't. He could see it. Feel it. But, hey, not his business, right?

She yawned again, then looked downright aggravated beneath the dark lenses. Surprising both of them, Trent reached out and tipped her shades up.

"Hey."

"You're exhausted."

"I'm fine."

"You're not." Guilt edged away a corner of anger. "Is worrying about me keeping you from sleeping?"

The look she slanted him had "duh" written all over it.

Growling, he strode two steps away, ran a hand through his hair, turned and came back. "Listen, I—"

She forestalled whatever he said with a shake of her head. "The last thing I want or deserve is your sympathy. Or your apology."

Her choice of words tweaked the protector within him. Deserve?

Jaden's voice interrupted them. "Hey, Mom. How's Cory?"

"All right. No fever right now."

The boy moved closer, his demeanor reflecting the struggle of leaving a great evening with new friends. Football-loving friends at that. "Do you want me to stop now so you can get home to her or can we stay a few minutes more?"

Trent added considerate to the list of Jaden's qualities.

"Grandma said she's sound asleep, so we're fine, honey. Keep playing."

Despite her weariness, she was willing to let him have time with new friends, learn new skills. Trent tried to find fault with that and couldn't, then put two and two together. "Somebody's sick? Besides your dad?"

"My little girl. She's three and I think the move wore her out. She caught back-to-back colds and it's taking a toll."

"On her and you."

Lyssa shrugged.

"Will she sleep tonight?"

"Who knows? Coughing kept her up last night. Hopefully tonight will be better."

"What's the doctor say?" he pressed.

Alyssa's hesitation said more than her easy words. "It's just a cold. Runny noses and coughs are part of childhood."

She didn't quite pull off the matter-of-fact attitude, but Trent left it alone. Not his problem. Still, he knew it couldn't be easy to come back east, move in with her parents, step into Gary's shoes at The Edge and deal with a sick kid.

And him.

But that was her fault for keeping him out of the picture for so long. He refused to feel sorry for that. So why did her next yawn punch a sympathy button he thought long-since buried?

It didn't, he assured himself. *No more than it would for anyone else.*

Darkness pushed the kids toward home a short while later. Trent met Jaden's look as the boy trotted their way, his easy lope inherent. "Tomorrow night?"

Jaden shook his head. "I work with Mom on Thursdays at the restaurant. Fridays, too. But I'm practicing with Coach Russo on Saturday afternoon. Can you come?"

"Wouldn't miss it for the world." His words hurt Alyssa. He saw that and did nothing to soften their blow. He'd already missed nearly a dozen years, time gone, irretrievable. Even if he'd planned something for Saturday, he'd forgo it to spend time with Jaden.

"Ready?" Addressing the question to Jaden, Alyssa ignored Trent.

So be it.

He nodded Jaden's way, headed to his car parked just in front of hers and shrugged off guilt that his words had been hurtful. After all, Trent figured it didn't even come close to evening the score in the retribution column. He started his sporty black coupe and headed away, trying to push the image of her tired eyes from his mind. The fact that he couldn't just intensified his anger.

Chapter Six

*D*ead.

Trent scowled at the Internet posting, sat back, then hunched forward again, his brain not comprehending what his eyes read in the two-year-old web clip from a southeast Montana newspaper.

> A one-car crash on Mueller Road claimed the life of an East Brogan man early Sunday morning. Vaughn Maxwell, 33, of Cuylerville was found dead in his vehicle during a routine patrol by the Cuyler County sheriff's office. Maxwell's car appeared to have veered off the road at high speed, hit a tree, rolled over and came to a sudden stop against another tree. Attempts to resuscitate the driver were unsuccessful. The Cuyler County coroner's office will conduct tests to see if alcohol use contributed to the crash.
>
> Maxwell is survived by his wife, Alyssa, stepson Jaden, and infant daughter Cory.

Shame coursed through him. He'd never checked Lyssa's status before coming back to Jamison, just a cursory look to make sure she was still in Montana. And she had been, at that time.

Obviously Gary's health concerns brought her east at the very same time he'd returned to help jump-start the job market.

But he'd stopped his query there, not wanting to be intrusive. Reading this Internet excerpt, he realized not only had she been alone for years, but she'd also been alone with two kids and not much family to speak of. He'd met Aunt Gee a long time ago. A sweet lady, lots of fun, but not big on family values. Although that may have changed, too, for all he knew. Obviously he was out of the loop where Alyssa's life was concerned.

Another thought occurred to him. Alyssa had no health insurance. That explained her hesitation the night before, the look of resignation when he questioned her about a doctor.

Would she be eligible for Social Security? Survivor benefits? And this Maxwell guy was old enough to be worth something before he died, wasn't he?

A series of government reclaim notices in the Cuyler County files told a different story. Vaughn Maxwell's property had been seized months after his death for failure to pay taxes and water rights violations. The official county claim gave no details about his displaced family, but from the figures he found on eastern Montana, hard times had fallen worse than they had in Jamison.

I'm glad she's here.

The thought both startled and comforted him. Better she be here among family and friends than so far away with no money, no home and no good prospects for employment.

Despite their history and her choices, he'd never wish her harm. Couldn't wish her harm. And the thought of how tired she looked bothered him.

But it shouldn't. She had her family now, her parents, their friends. A home. A place of her own.

Not exactly, his conscience prodded. *Living with Mom and Dad at age thirty probably isn't a cakewalk.*

Because Trent hadn't had the opportunity to live with a mother or father in nearly thirty years, the concept was lost on him. He'd never experienced that dream, to be part of a loving family he was actually related to.

He loved his foster parents, a kind family who'd relocated to North Carolina years ago. Their two children, both older than him. But despite their kindness and goodness, it wasn't the same. He knew that. Felt it. Always a tad different, set apart.

But now he had Jaden. For the first time in nearly three decades Trent had a living, breathing, bona fide member of his family nearby, a dream come true.

He stared at the online image of Vaughn Maxwell, trying to determine the kind of man he'd been. High speed, possible alcohol use...

That combination said a lot about a man in his thirties with a wife and two kids.

He hoped he was kind. Nice. The thought of this guy barreling down a country road under the influence made that seem unlikely. Either way, the man was dead and buried, leaving Alyssa and two kids with a pile of bills that couldn't be paid. She lost her husband and had her house taken from her in the space of a few short months. Rough time line.

She could have come back. Her parents would have helped.

Trent paused.

He knew Gary. Lyssa's father might resemble a teddy bear, but his grizzled manner soon set a person straight. Pragmatic, tough and focused, he took a bulldog stance when approaching a problem. Effective in business, not so much in family. Was that reason enough to stay away?

The phone rang. He answered it, one eye on the screen. "Trent Michaels."

"Tom Dewey here, Trent. How soon can I expect your bid?"

The phone call he'd been prepping for. Tom Dewey was NWAC, Naval Warfare Air Command, a military man and commander who fully appreciated Trent's upgraded magnetron design for this radar system. A good man who wasn't afraid to go out on a limb.

"I'm finishing up the specs and overnighting it to you first thing in the morning. Soon enough?"

"Perfect. We just got a bid in from Davison in Maryland and while they're good, I'd like to see some of these bids go to areas with more economic challenge going on. With Walker's strong track record on small contracts, Helen's already got a foot in the door."

"That explains your encouragement when the economic preference bill went up before Congress," Trent noted.

"Exactly. I'll be watching for the bid. And don't be afraid to follow it up with others if Walker can handle the workload. We're not in a hurry, but we're not good at waiting games either."

Trent knew that firsthand. Military wheels dragged in some cases, but when push came to shove, things could happen in an instant. "We'll be ready for whatever comes our way, Tom. You have my word."

"Well, good. Nice talking to you."

"And you."

Trent hung up the phone, closed the web page concerning Vaughn Maxwell and refocused his attentions on the bid. He was here to do a job, to meet his goal of procuring new and long-lasting employment for the community. He needed to be at the top of his game, unfettered by past or present.

He refilled his coffee mug and settled into his chair, reconfiguring estimates and numbers until he was satisfied long hours later. The bid was tight, accurate and hard-hitting where it needed to be. Once they had a successful track record with various military units, he could afford to be less stringent. But not now when being passed over could spell the downfall of a grassroots company refitting their manufacturing to meet the needs of a contract that might not come.

Trent refused to let that happen.

"Mommy, can I come, too?" Cory's plaintive voice trailed as Alyssa loaded the back of the car with her mother's strudels on Saturday morning. An Edge mainstay, the cheese, apple and triple-berry melt-in-your-mouth texture of the fresh pastries provided a sweet touch to end a meal or as the base layer of an Edge favorite, super strudel sundaes.

Alyssa nodded toward the backseat. "Sure you can. Hop in. Do you need help with your buckles?"

"I'm fwee," Cory reminded her, her right hand displaying three tiny fingers that looked suspiciously sticky. "I'm big."

"That you are, sugarplum. All right, have at it and then you and I will take these up the hill."

Cory's endearing smile sent a pang of regret through Alyssa. The past two weeks had been incredibly hectic, and Cory's bright acceptance of a little time with Mommy cut deep.

"Alyssa, can you take these up as well?" Susan came across the yard with a large box of silk florals, the bright summer tones magnified by the morning sun, birdsong and the sheen of dew dampening her sneakers.

"Sure. We'll put them back here." Alyssa opened the wide tailgate of her mother's SUV and whistled appreciation. "I love driving this thing. Total power rush."

Susan laughed. "While I prefer your little car. Except on snowy winter days. Then this four-wheel-drive monster becomes my new best friend."

"I can imagine. I'm taking Cory with me."

"Shopping?"

Alyssa shook her head. Cory needed new summer clothes but they weren't in the budget yet. Alyssa kept her gaze averted. "Next week. Today we're just dropping this off at the restaurant and maybe a trip to the playground if Cory's super-duper good."

"I will be, Mommy. I pwomise this much." Cory spread her arms wide, her sincere look matching her tone.

"Prrrrrrromise," Alyssa corrected, stressing the R sound.

Cory nodded. "Pwwwwwwwwwwwomise!"

"Good girl."

Susan exchanged a grin with Alyssa. "She sounds just like you did at the same age. A little trouble with R's and L's."

"Really?" Her mother's assertion pleased Alyssa. She had a hard time seeing much of herself in either child and that just seemed wrong after nine months of pregnancy. On the other hand, considering the way she'd mucked up her life, maybe taking after others was a good thing. "I'll be back later then. Rocco's doing afternoon/evening like always and I'm closing."

Rocco was the head cook at The Edge, a tough-as-nails, my-way-or-the-highway–type guy. Her mother moved forward, her voice soft. "Is he still giving you a hard time?"

If by hard time her mother meant was Rocco an overbearing chauvinist jerk, then the answer would be an overwhelming yes. Still the cook knew his stuff and Alyssa couldn't afford histrionics in the kitchen. Rocco's fits were renowned and Alyssa didn't have the time to mollify him like her father would.

Or the guts, but that was a different story. "Rocco's Rocco. I just stay out of his way."

Guilt stuck in her craw.

Wasn't that exactly what she'd tried to do with Vaughn? Mollify things once they'd gone bad and stay out of his way? Self-recriminating memories churned inside her. If she'd stood her ground and left Vaughn when she should have…

She felt gutless for good reason. Standing her ground didn't come naturally. She'd been a mouse, quiet and cowering long past the time when she should have made a stand. If she had, things might be different now.

Shame cut again.

She'd done everything she could to make sure Jaden didn't suspect his stepfather's temper. That meant no crying, no begging, but it was a small price to pay to protect Jaden's formative years. And Vaughn had changed after Cory's birth, her sweet, baby face giving him something to work for, to build for until another financial bad turn brought him down shortly after her first birthday.

She caught her breath, refusing to revisit those months, hindsight clarifying what seemed so muddled then.

Get out. Save your children.

If she'd only had the courage to do that sooner...

But she didn't and there would always be a gap in her heart, a chasm, a small yawning space that could never quite be filled.

She'd made up her mind she'd never be fooled again, that she'd never be the object of another man's anger. Vaughn's crash put an end to that bout of craziness, but financial ruin brought its own share of troubles.

She was stronger now. She knew that. Made sure of it.

And right now Rocco's finesse in the kitchen was important to the well-being of her family, her father's health and their restaurant. She wasn't about to do anything to mess with that, not after a long, tough winter.

"I'll be back later. Jaden's practicing this afternoon."

"With Chris and Trent. I remember."

Susan's upthrust brow showed her concern, but she said nothing more.

"Bye, Gwammy!"

"Goodbye, sugarplum. I'll see you in a little while, okay?"

"'Kay."

Susan sent Alyssa a sideways glance and kept her voice low. "She's wide awake now."

"And then some. The cold and the move must have really tuckered her out."

"I'll say."

They'd had to wake Cory up the last several mornings, long after her normal greet-the-sun rising. And her afternoon naps were elongated as well, but Alyssa knew illness and change taxed little ones. Now that they were here and almost settled, Cory would have time to relax, be the preschooler she was meant to be.

Chapter Seven

Alyssa dropped off the boxed strudels, double checked the staff to make sure the luncheon shift was well-covered for a gorgeous spring Saturday, then headed down to the village where a castle playground anchored the southwest corner of their town park. She grabbed a water bottle, opened Cory's door and nodded encouragement as Cory's little fingers finagled the release tab. When Alyssa reached in to help, Cory shook her head, chin thrust out, brow tight. "I can do it."

"Okay."

Alyssa drew back, patient. Cory was such an easygoing child that quests for independence were broadly encouraged. Long moments later, a tiny click spelled success. "I did it!"

"You did, clever girl. Good job." Alyssa closed the door and motioned toward the playground with her head. "Ready?"

"Oh, yes."

Excitement tremored her tone. In the bright sun, the shadows beneath Cory's eyes seemed deeper, more pronounced, violet smudges against porcelain skin. But her nose wasn't running any longer, and the cough had gone from chronic to occasional. Day-by-day she was regaining her normal strength and tone.

Cory dashed across the crushed gravel, pigtails flying, her eyes on the tall, spiraling castle tower.

Of course.

Alyssa moved at a slower pace, watching Cory's progress until the little girl's saucy grin peered down from the wooden rail. "Look, Mommy! I'm way up here!"

"You are. Good job, sugarplum. Now how do you plan to get down?"

"Over the bwidge."

"Ooooo…" Alyssa nodded to show she was impressed. "The very wiggly, rickety bridge?"

"Yes."

"Good luck."

"Fank you."

Alyssa grinned. Obviously the *th* sound needed tweaking as well. She watched as Cory tested the wood with one foot, the suspension bridge designed to wiggle and jiggle beneath busy feet. Gripping the handrails, Cory put foot after foot until she swung up into a turret on the opposite end. "I did it!"

"Wonderful."

"Can you play wif me, Mommy?"

"Sure." Alyssa set the water bottle down, crawled through a space that obviously wasn't designed for a woman's build, and worked her way to the upper level through a series of tunnels. Just before the top, she called Cory's name, teasing her.

"Where are you, Mommy?"

"I'm stuck."

Cory giggled.

"I need help," Alyssa continued, pumping desperation into her tone.

Cory giggled again. "I fink you're kidding me."

"Help." Alyssa stuck a hand up through the tunnel, waving it wildly.

Cory laughed out loud. "I will help you." She scampered back across the bridge, grabbed Alyssa's fingers and pulled. "Come on, Mommy."

Alyssa pretended to try. "Not working. I appear to be too big."

"Reawwy?" Cory tugged again, then approached the problem

with all the innocence of a small child. "Mister Man? Can you help get my mommy out? She's stuck."

Mister Man?

Cory was calling a stranger for help.

Alyssa wriggled through the last stretch of tunnel, but her capri pocket snagged a post. She had to wiggle back down to free the fold of material, then back up, thoughts of Cory calling out to a perfect stranger spurring her to fumble. "Cory."

"You need help?"

No.

Oh, no.

She stared up into Trent's face, a hint of humor softening the glare that had marked their initial meetings. "No, I'm fine, actually. I was just…" She tried to pull herself up and out of the tunnel, but the cuff caught once more. Biting her lip she wriggled down, undid the cuff again and shifted back up.

Yup. Trent was still there, Cory alongside him. Her little girl tapped his arm. "Mister Man can help you."

Before Alyssa could protest, Trent caught her beneath the arms and pulled.

The fact that she slid forward easily made him frown. She stood, shook her clothes into place, decided she'd never wear anything with cuffs again and faced him. "I wasn't really stuck." She nodded Cory's way. "We were playing a game."

"But you were," Cory protested. She grabbed Trent's arm and stared up into his face, imploring. "I pulled and pulled, but I couldn't get her out. You wescued her."

"Glad to be of service," Trent murmured wryly. His glance scanned the tunnel and her hips. His lips twitched. "And it appears you may have been stuck for some time if I hadn't answered the young lady's call for help."

Great. Add fat to her list of daily problems because her girth was too wide to make it through a playground tunnel. "My cuff caught the edge," she told him, not ready to concede a width problem. "And I was teasing her. I could have gotten out anytime."

"Uh-huh."

"Wight, Mommy." Cory's look of disbelief joined Trent's. She stepped forward, her little face sincere. "It's okay to ask for help when you need it, wight?"

Wonderful. The kid was throwing her words back at her. Alyssa decided the high road offered a better tactical choice for the moment. "Right. And you did help me, but you're not supposed to talk to strangers without Mommy, are you?"

Cory frowned in confusion and waved a hand. "But you were wight there."

"Good point, kid." Trent crouched to Cory's level. "And I think you were a very brave little girl to want to rescue your mommy."

Cory dimpled. "Fank you, Mister Man."

"Trent." Trent offered his hand in introduction. "You can call me Trent."

"And you can call me Cory," she answered happily. "And now we can be fwiends."

"Cory…"

"I'd like that," Trent interrupted. "I'm going to play football with your big brother this afternoon, so it would be good for you and me to be friends I think."

"You play with Jay?"

Trent nodded. "We both like football."

"Jay wuvs football." Cory nodded, still clasping Trent's hand, the visual knifing Alyssa's heart, the tiny hand clinging to the much bigger, burlier one. "Mommy says he eats, bweathes and sweeps football."

"I do say that, don't I?" Alyssa smiled at the little girl's fervor. "And I better watch what I say, sugarplum, if you're going to repeat me verbatim."

Trent stood but didn't release Cory's hand. "You're okay? Really?" His glance to the tunnel and his tone showed genuine concern.

Alyssa stepped back from the note of kindness. "Fine. You were running?" She swept his shorts and T-shirt a glance. "You run every day?"

"Every day I can. When your job changes from directing troops to sitting at a desk, it's not easy to stay in shape."

Seriously?

From Alyssa's vantage point, Trent appeared to be in prime physical condition—broad shoulders tapering to a wide, barreled chest above a nipped waist, the white cotton T-shirt and running shorts accenting military muscle. Therefore she made it a point not to look.

Mostly.

She cleared her throat and directed her gaze to Cory. "We have ten more minutes of playtime. Then we've got to get home. I've got laundry to do before I go to work. And stuff to move into the new apartment."

A group of small children entered the playground from below. Cory turned, hopeful. Alyssa nodded their way. "Yes, go ahead. I'll be at the picnic table watching."

"Fanks, Mommy!"

Trent eyed the upper reaches of the playground, then moved toward the slide. "It seems there's only one way down."

The tunnel slide curled and curved toward the ground. Alyssa frowned and nodded. "Yup. Bad choice of clothing on my part."

"Why?"

"Brush burns." She pointed to the slide. "It's not so bad for little kids, but grown-ups weigh more. When we slide down these plastic tunnels, we bump."

"Ah." He stepped forward, gallant as always. "I'll take the first hit."

She smiled and saw his eyes note that, his gaze rest lightly on hers, the animosity she'd noted their last few meetings softened by... something. He slid down, bellowed a few loud ouches and ohs for her benefit, then stood grinning from the ground below. "Your turn."

Was it the thought of her getting pummeled by the slide that sparked his grin or was he just trying to cajole a laugh out of her?

Like he did so long ago.

She quashed that thought. She'd done the unthinkable in his eyes, and it would be in her best interests to remember that. She deliberately stifled a small yip and a growl as she tumbled to the graveled ground below, the slide taking no small share of skin along the outside edge of her right calf.

He caught her at the bottom, stood her upright, gave her a once-over and shrugged. "You survived."

She resisted the urge to rub her calf. "Piece of cake."

"Uh-huh."

The humor in his eyes said otherwise, but he let it slide. Cory was in the midst of kids on the swings, her legs bicycling furiously, trying to pump. Trent laughed and jogged her way, took a spot behind her and said, "Allow me." Two brawny arms that looked as if they saw a weight room daily pushed her with a force that set the other children begging.

Alyssa watched as he sidestepped, avoiding backswing as he pushed one child, then another. When Alyssa took her spot at the picnic table, an expectant young mother nodded to the swings. "Your husband's a doll for doing that. I'm due anytime and I sat here hoping they wouldn't ask, and then he stepped in. A Godsend, for sure."

Alyssa cringed. "Um, thank you, but he's not my husband."

"Ah."

The other woman's look softened to say she understood that modern-day relationships weren't always by the book. If only Alyssa's life had proven that simple. She shook her head and leaned closer. "I'm a widow. That's my little girl, Cory. And that's…" she hesitated, choosing words with care "…our friend Trent."

"Nice friend." The woman's tone and grin said she wasn't too old or too pregnant not to appreciate Trent's more obvious characteristics.

Heat climbed Alyssa's neck and cheeks.

"And he's good with kids," the other gal observed, cranking a sideways look toward Alyssa. "Might be something you want to consider for further reference before half the singles in Allegany County get a look at him. We're talking seriously sweet."

Alyssa laughed. "It's not like that."

"Oh, honey, it never is," the other woman agreed, stretching out her hand. "Until it *is*, of course. I'm Ginger Baxter. And you are?"

"Alyssa Langley. My parents own The Edge."

Ginger nodded. "We've had your dad on the prayer list at Holy Name for several weeks, and my husband and I love to go up the hill to The Edge for special occasions. Such a lovely place."

"Thank you."

"In fact," Ginger continued, "we were thinking about having Dad's anniversary there."

"Your parents?"

"No," Ginger explained. "Forty years in the ministry." She waved a hand toward the town circle, the centered parklike median surrounded by quaint country churches, the pastoral setting post-card perfect. "I'm Reverend Hannity's daughter."

Alyssa frowned. "Reverend Hannity doesn't have a daughter." She'd been around long enough to watch the Hannitys bury their only son, a little boy who died of bone cancer a long time ago.

Ginger splayed her hands as if the facts spoke for themselves. "He did. My mother didn't like life in the ministry, so she divorced him early on. Never told him about me."

The parallel jabbed Alyssa's gut.

"I found him once I was grown. I came to town, realized my mother was right, that small towns and ministers are a royal pain, that there's way too much of everyone knowing everyone else's business and being from a city, I wasn't used to that. I figured I'd head on down the road the first chance I got."

Alyssa smiled, noting her pregnant belly. "And?"

"God had other plans. I fell head over heels in love with a minister who came to town determined not to find a wife."

Alyssa laughed and quoted, "You wanna hear God laugh?"

"Tell him your plans," Ginger finished. "Exactly. So now I have my father preaching on one side of the circle," she waved a hand toward the sweet white church, "and my husband on the opposite side." This time the hand pointed toward the cream-and-taupe–stoned church front. "I'm completely surrounded. What's a girl to do?"

"You caved."

"Totally. And I couldn't be happier. Although I'd love to see my toes again."

"Understandable."

Ginger stood and stretched, her gaze down rueful. "Three more weeks."

"Twenty-one long days. Give or take."

"Amen." Ginger stretched out her hand again. "Alyssa, good meeting you. And our little girls look to be about the same age. If you want to get together so they can play, give me a call. And if you don't," she warned with a teasing grin, "I'll call you. Ministers' wives are nothing if not slightly obnoxious and intrusive. It balances all the things my husband can't do because he's bound by rules of propriety."

Alyssa laughed out loud. "I'd love to. I haven't had time to meet up with any old friends since I've come back, and Cory needs kids to play with."

"An only child?"

Alyssa bit back a sigh and shook her head. "No, I have an older son. But eleven-year-old boys limit the time they spend with dolls and My Little Ponies."

"As well they should." Ginger whistled for her crew, rolled her eyes when they ignored her and headed toward the swings. "I'll call. We'll set something up. I'm sure you're working hard at The Edge, but that's mostly nights, right?"

"Yes."

"Perfect." She flashed a thank-you smile to Trent, gathered her three older kids and headed down the road. At the park's edge, the kids turned, hollered their thanks, then raced for home while Ginger followed at a more leisured pace.

Well…waddled, actually.

"Mommy, I had so much fun!" Color brightened Cory's face,

her morning pallor erased by exertion. "Twent, you are a very good pusher!"

"Thank you." He hoisted Cory as if she weighed nothing, tweaked her nose to elicit a giggle, then set her down. An awkward quiet ensued, until Alyssa broke it with a shrug. "That was Reverend Hannity's daughter."

Trent frowned. "He doesn't have a daughter."

"It seems he does."

"But—"

"Come on, sugarplum, we've got to get home so Mommy can get stuff done." Alyssa lifted Cory and rubbed noses with her, the little girl's glee contagious. "You can help me fold towels and things."

"But not my ni-ni," the little girl implored.

"Your blanket," Alyssa corrected, trying to encourage Cory to give baby talk a rest.

Trent moved closer. "Another language, I take it?"

"Yeah, kid-speak. Her soft, fuzzy pink blanket with pink satin edging is her night-night blanket. Somehow that got reduced to ni-ni."

"A sensible abbreviation in my mind, Miss Cory."

She grinned up at him. "Fank you. I love my ni-ni."

Alyssa shot him a look as she headed toward the car. "We can't wash it when Miss Cory is awake because she'll stand guard at the washing machine, watching and waiting the whole time."

Trent paused, imagining how sweet that sounded, a small child hovering in the laundry room, counting down minutes until her security blanket was clean, warm and dry. The thought that he'd never been able to enjoy a moment like that with his son pushed him to take a firm step back. "Thanks for playing with me, Cory."

She beamed and reached out to give him a hug.

Talk about awkward.

Alyssa was holding her, and if he hugged her, well… it would almost be like he was hugging Alyssa.

Alyssa read his hesitation. A look of guilty understanding

flashed across her features. She set Cory down. The little girl gave Trent a big hug, dipping her soft cheek into his neck, her wispy hair smelling of shampoo and maple syrup. Pancakes for breakfast, he assumed. The thought made him grin, imagining the talkative little girl getting syrup in her hair, down her chin, on her sleeve. He set her down, bent low and kissed her cheek. "You have a good day, okay?"

"I will." Her head bobbed with enthusiasm as she climbed into the car. "You, too!"

"Thank you, Cory."

Alyssa rounded the car to the driver's side. Trent watched her move, her glossy dark hair reflecting the warming sun. He wondered if it still got a hint of red in the summertime. If it would still slip through his fingers like spun silk, the soft sheen inborn, not product-induced.

Stop. Now.

Right then he thanked God for a good conscience, a steady reminder to help keep him focused, on track. Yes, she was beautiful. She always had been. But she'd deceived him, causing him a grievous loss, the first eleven years of his son's life.

An unforgivable action.

Trent didn't lie or cheat and rarely hedged unless the absolute truth would get him into trouble…and those decisions were made on a case-by-case basis and generally involved women and clothing.

But he was an officer and a gentleman, trained by the best of the best. He didn't take that consignment lightly.

Alyssa faced him once she opened her door. "Thanks for playing with her." She nodded toward the village churches where Ginger's older kids played around their yard, their excited shouts filling the warm spring air. "And them."

"And for rescuing you."

She faced him square, her expression carefully blank. "An unnecessary inconvenience. Sorry."

He should have left it at that. Let her climb into the car and drive back up the hill to her parents' place, chalking this up to just another happenstance meeting, a circumstance destined because of their proximity.

But he couldn't. He gripped the top of the car and leaned forward, facing her. "I wasn't inconvenienced."

His intensity unnerved her. She paled. Her mouth opened slightly, her smoke-hazel eyes searching his. Then she swallowed hard and climbed into the car.

He watched as she drove away, the SUV sparkling in the bright sun, the new leaves too tiny to offer much shade. As the SUV circled the green, Trent brought to mind every possible reason for avoiding contact if being around her produced this effect.

Sharing a son negated all of them. Simple mathematics would thrust them together from this point forward. The trick was, how would he handle the mixed crush of feelings she inspired by simply being Alyssa. His first love.

Your only love.

Yeah, well. That thought pushed him into dangerous how-stupid-can-one-man-be territory, and Trent had no intention of going there. Once fooled, shame on you. Twice fooled, shame on me. The old saying packed a punch of common sense.

Trent glanced at his runner's watch, eyed the village and trotted toward Good Shepherd Church. He wanted to reconnect with Reverend Hannity, a man who'd always encouraged him as a boy. He could use a dose of that wisdom about now.

Chapter Eight

"Trent."

Reverend Hannity put aside the morning paper and strode across the backyard, his gait a touch slower but his welcome smile unchanged. "Welcome home."

Trent seized the offered hand and shook it, then clasped the older man in a hug. "Thank you, sir."

"Come over, sit down. Pamela was just putting a fresh pot of coffee on. You'll have some, won't you?"

"I'd love some."

Mrs. Hannity waved from the kitchen window, a dishcloth flapping in the air, a Betty Crocker housewife in a time when Betty got nudged aside in favor of Stouffer's. She bustled out a moment later, her apron clean and neat this early in the day. Trent knew it wouldn't stay that way. The plate of cookies she set down before she hugged him offered proof. Mrs. Hannity loved to bake, loved to cook, and her ample proportions lent mute testimony to both. "Trent, you look wonderful!"

Trent grinned and nodded. The kindly pastor's wife talked in exclamation points, her uplifting excitement contagious and uncontainable, a perfect complement to her husband's calm demeanor. They were Frick and Frack, salt and pepper, and they'd been together for over thirty years. Trent found that amazing and inspiring. A goal to strive for.

"And look at you, all grown up! Such a fine young man! And back home with us! The reverend and I are just so happy to hear it…"

"Thank you." He slanted a glance to the cookies, then back to her. "I must admit, there are few things I've missed more than your cookies."

She laughed, delighted.

"And thank you for all the times you shipped them to me, all over the world. The guys and I appreciated each and every one."

"Oh, you." She flushed, embarrassed, flapped her apron and looked for all the world like a blushing teen. "You boys enjoy your coffee. I've got things going in the kitchen."

"Thank you, dear." The reverend sent her a smile meant for her and only her, even after all these years. As she hurried back across the yard, he reached forward, snagged a cookie and bit into it with obvious relish. "A good woman's hand in the kitchen is a wonderful thing, son. A true gift from God."

"Luckily I learned to cook in the service." Trent settled down across from him and didn't miss the older man's look of assessment.

"Not the same thing, boy, not even close, but we'll let that slide for the moment. You've come back to help, I hear."

"Yes." Trent sipped his coffee and leaned forward. "When I realized how quickly the economy here had gone downhill, I knew I had to do whatever I could to change things. I have the expertise and the education to make this happen. With a little luck and God's blessing."

"With God's blessing you shouldn't need the luck. And with Helen's backing, you should be fine. It's going all right?"

Trent made a face, then nodded. "Fine. The work aspects anyway."

"And the personal?"

Leave it to Reverend Hannity to get right to the point. Trent sighed, sipped his coffee and gazed beyond the small, quaint rectory to the churchyard. "You know?"

"Yes."

"She told you?"

The reverend shook his head. "She hasn't come to church or stopped by. No, I knew the minute I laid eyes on him and that explained so much."

Trent frowned.

"Why she never came back. Why her father sounded defensive every time her name was mentioned. Why Susan bore an inexplicable sadness in her eyes. But no one spoke of it, or addressed the issue until Gary's heart attack a few weeks ago." He sighed. "With business bad all around, there was no way he could close the restaurant while he recovered. And Susan needed to be able to take care of him. Luckily, Alyssa was available to step in, but at no small cost to her."

Trent's frown deepened. "That's a generous way of looking at it."

"Whereas I'd say practical." The reverend sipped his coffee and faced Trent, thoughtful. "Knowing Alyssa like I do, I think her altruistic nature got the better of her. Pushed her to be the martyr for your sake."

"She didn't have the right to keep the pregnancy a secret," Trent countered. "He was my child, too."

"I'm not arguing that you are a wronged party, but you are not the *only* wronged party here." The reverend leaned closer. "Alyssa sacrificed a lot—including her pristine image—to have your child, and she still managed to raise him to be a fine boy. I'm simply saying that with your military tactical education, you need to be able to sort the forest from the trees. Step outside yourself and view the whole picture."

Trent nodded, the older man's words spiking what his conscience had prodded the other day. He'd gotten a tiny view of what Alyssa's life had been like the past several years, and it wasn't pretty. Here she had a chance to start again, begin anew.

He considered that thought, then sighed. "This isn't easy. Any of it."

The older man read his expression and laughed. "God didn't

put women on earth to make things easy for us but to make things better for us. And his instructions on that were quite explicit: *Husbands, love your wives as Christ loved the church*.... Sacrificial love. Sanctified love."

"Alyssa's not my wife."

"But she is the mother of your child. At some point in time you had deep feelings for her. High regard."

Those words pricked Trent's moral bubble. "If I'd had higher regard, we wouldn't be in this situation."

"And Jaden wouldn't exist." The reverend shrugged. "You were young and in love. Those emotions and feelings are hard to keep in check. But what's done is done. Now the trick is to find common ground and move forward, with the boy's best interests at heart."

"I'm selfish enough to have struggled with that." Trent's admission eased part of the ache inside him. "I wanted to shout it from the mountaintops, claim him and run off with him. Give Alyssa a taste of what it feels like to be sucker punched like this."

"But you didn't."

"She talked me out of it."

"Oh?"

How could a man put so much into one little word? Trent grimaced. "She made me look at it from Jaden's point of view."

"A wise mother."

Trent's frown deepened. "In some ways. In others?" He paused and shrugged. "She had choices she could have made that would have ensured a more stable life for her. For him. Once I was out of the academy, the question of parenting was moot."

"And have you asked why she chose as she did?"

"Not yet."

"Then wait on your judgment until you know all the facts. She was young when she left." The reverend shrugged again. "Young people make mistakes. And with no support, guilt can compound those mistakes."

Didn't Trent know that firsthand? Hadn't he stepped out far

too freely once he'd graduated as a commissioned officer? Oh, he'd been around the block a few times before his conscience and faith recentered. Could Alyssa have regrets like that?

Possibly.

Enough to keep her away?

Trent imagined Gary's disappointment in his daughter's mistakes. He could only imagine what things must have been like for her to admit her pregnancy as a teen and face her parents on her own. He should have been there, by her side, sparing her as best he could. He was just as much to blame as she…more so because he was a man who believed in upholding women.

She'd sacrificed a lot for him. It didn't make her choices right but understandable. Trent sighed and ran a finger around the upper edge of his coffee mug. "I'll talk to her. And I'll go see Gary."

"He's been ill," Reverend Hannity cautioned. "It might not be a bad idea to wait a few days."

"I don't intend to upset him, but reassure him." Trent sat straighter and met the reverend's gaze. "Twelve years too late, but better late than never."

"Would you like me to accompany you?"

Trent shook his head. "No. God's got my back. Gary might hit hard and low, but he has every right to have his say. Until we do that, I don't see much hope to move on."

The reverend stood, rounded the table and embraced Trent. "I'm adding wisdom to your list of attributes. If you need me…"

"I know where to find you." Trent started away, then turned, eyeing the large sign in front of the church, the outline of a roof nearly filled in, money increments marked along the left side. "We need a new roof."

"And the youth rooms patched and painted where the water leaks damaged the drywall and ceilings. And a new carpet in the back wing. We're starting next week. Can you join us? Pamela's heading up the food committee."

Trent grinned. "Reason enough right there." He nodded toward the stone church across the green. "And since when do you have a daughter?"

The reverend's smile brightened. "You met Ginger?"

"Sort of. In the park. I met the kids," he added, smiling. "Great bunch."

"They are that, and another on the way. Mother and I have a great time spoiling them."

Trent had no trouble believing that. "Where did she come from?"

"My first wife."

Trent frowned.

"We married when I was newly out of seminary. I was young. Stupid. Fairly naive about women, about men."

"You?" Disbelief colored Trent's tone. The reverend had always seemed wise and unencumbered.

"Yes, me. I didn't know then what a husband should be to a wife. I could quote chapter and verse, but I didn't live what I preached. And we lived in a small town, a tiny place not unlike Jamison."

Trent nodded.

"Janice was a city girl. A college graduate from a well-to-do family. Putting her in a small, closely knit town drove her crazy. She said she felt claustrophobic because she couldn't do anything without someone watching."

"Somewhat true."

"And devastating to her. She left, divorced me and had Ginger unbeknownst to me. When Ginger showed up ten years ago, I was furious that her mother thought so little of me that she kept our daughter hidden away."

The similarities to his situation spoke volumes. He swallowed hard. "Did you forgive her?"

"Yes and no. Janice died when Ginger was in middle school, leaving her to be raised by a stepfather, rather than tell Ginger the truth. I forgave her leaving and her deception, but her secrecy beyond death was harder to reconcile. Ginger had a right to know me. Know us." He waved a hand to the kitchen.

The dishcloth waved back.

The reverend's jaw softened. "But from bad comes wondrous good. If I hadn't married Janice, Mother and I wouldn't have Ginger living across the way now. With a pile of grandchildren for us to enjoy. We wouldn't have the Christmas mornings and birthday afternoons that we enjoy so much. Since we had Kevin for so little time—"

Their little boy, taken so young. Trent remembered the collective sadness within the town, mourning the minister's loss.

"Having Ginger's crew underfoot seems like the second chance we always longed for."

Second chances. A great concept. Difficult to manage. Trent clapped the older man on the back. "It will all work out, I know. I'm just a little overcome by being in the middle of a drama I didn't know I created."

"Welcome to life." The reverend grinned across the way to where a medium-sized boy dribbled a soccer ball in and around his mother's rose bushes. "I'm going to take that boy to the park to practice and save him from his mother's wrath if he ruins her flower bed when she's this pregnant."

"Wise move."

The reverend grinned. "That's the plus of being a minister and a man. I can read boys well."

Trent couldn't argue with that. Hadn't the reverend always been a steadfast supporter? Watching the older man loop an arm around the boy, Trent remembered how often the minister made time for him.

So he'd forgiven his ex-wife. Mostly.

What sounded easy wasn't. Despite the reverend's kind words, Trent recognized his internal struggle.

Father, you've blessed me often. You gave me family when I had none. You gave me food, shelter and warmth. You gave me a community that opened their arms, hearts and wallets to care for me.

Soften my heart. Soothe my soul. In my head I know what's done is done, but then I backtrack to what-if's.

Strengthen me, God, to be the man I imagined myself to be until I was tested.

His first step toward being that stronger man was to see Gary Langley and ask forgiveness. He'd approach Gary while Alyssa and Jaden were working later. A glance at his watch said he'd better hustle home and change if he wanted to be on time to meet Chris and Jaden in the park.

The thought of another round of football with his son lent its own inspiration.

From bad came wondrous good.

Reverend Hannity's words comforted, their simple sensibility a balm to his soul. He waved to the reverend as he passed the park, the older man demonstrating skills to his attentive grandson, a Norman Rockwell glimpse of Americana. Sweet. Poignant. Perfect.

The fact that it hadn't started off perfect only made it that much better.

Chapter Nine

Alyssa noted the white stretch limousine as it leisurely drove through town, horn-honking, a happy bridal party waving out the windows, their joy contagious.

A part of her wondered how sweet it would be to have that kind of wedding—the joy, the pomp, the circumstance.

Another part wrote it off as an impracticality that promised little. The proof was in the pudding, and by her experience, marriage left a lot to be desired.

But her practical side pushed her to view weddings from a business standpoint. If only The Edge could garner a share of the wedding industry. People married even in tough economic times, and if she could plan a way to facilitate wedding receptions at a reasonable cost and decent profit, the six-month wedding season could provide enough capital to keep the restaurant solvent through the harshest winter.

Her brain churned possibilities as she pulled around to the small staff parking area. The beautiful morning held true to a gorgeous afternoon, and despite being off-hours, the restaurant was bustling. That meant Rocco probably needed supper prep help first thing, and since Cat was on the later shift, she knew the front end was well in hand. And Jaden would come over later to bus tables, helping the waitstaff on what she hoped would be a cranking busy Saturday night.

"No pasta."

Rocco's bark attacked the moment she walked in the door. She swiped her hoodie onto a hook, grabbed a full apron from the box near the door, tugged it on and moved forward. "What do you mean? I ordered it."

"They send this." He held a ten-pound box of pasta aloft. "I no cook this." He pronounced "this" as if the pasta was so far beneath his level as to be summarily dismissed.

Please.

Alyssa reached out a hand.

Rocco refused to give up the package, his theatrics unfinished. "Many years I work for your father, a good man. He never buy Rocco *this*."

Again the emphasis. Talk about overdone.

Welcome to Saturday.

Alyssa stepped around him, pulled out the invoice from the local distributor and scanned the first page, found the item, then nodded. "They back-ordered the Barilla and substituted this brand for today." She tapped the invoice. "It's right here."

Her tone said he could have read it for himself and spared everyone the drama. His expression said he didn't like her attitude or her stance.

Oh, well.

She wasn't out to pick a fight with Rocco, but she'd promised herself to never back down from a man again. That included here and now, regardless of how necessary he was to a seamless dinner rush.

Rocco leaned in, aggression darkening his face. "I no use this."

"We have Alfredo on the menu for tonight. It's a local favorite, and while I love Barilla pasta, I can't change the fact that the supplier ran out."

He scowled as she withdrew her cell phone. "But I can call in the reserves." She punched in the assistant cook's number, and when he answered, she asked, "Jim, Atlas sent us the wrong pasta. Can you swing by Tops Market on your way in and pick us up all the Barilla fettuccine and linguine they have on the shelves? If they have an extra case in stock, better yet."

"Sure. I'm leaving in five minutes, so I'll be there shortly."

"Awesome. Thank you."

She repocketed the phone and faced Rocco. "Done."

He didn't look appeased but that was his problem, not hers. And she knew he could have called Jim himself, that he waited deliberately because Gary's choices hurt his feelings. Her father had called her home to help instead of assigning the burly cook to oversee the restaurant in Gary's absence, but Alyssa had been in the food business long enough to know that not many cooks could walk the line of successful business management on the dining room floor. Finessing unhappy customers took patience and humor, qualities Rocco didn't possess.

No, her father had done the right thing. She knew it. What's more, Rocco knew it. He just didn't like it.

Wanting peace, she checked the cooler, saw that the crabmeat casseroles were ready to be warmed and served, that the basic salad mix was prepped, and the soups were complete and wafting mixed aromas of mushroom and garlic throughout the area.

Wonderful.

"I'll finish the twice-baked potatoes over here."

Rocco scowled, refused to answer and muttered under his breath as he crossed to the front of the kitchen. With the increasing warmth outside, the kitchen temps would rise accordingly. Dealing with Rocco and the rising heat should be a test of patience and fortitude.

Or license to kill.

She'd strive for the former and try to look for the good in Rocco. While his cooking abilities were unquestionable, his animosity to his team had caused problems in the past. The fact that he thought he could get away with that with Alyssa running things in Gary's absence said he neither liked nor respected her.

Again, his problem, not hers. She'd do her job and do it well, despite his negativity. He obviously wanted her to fail. She was just as determined to do well, the restaurant business as natural to her as breathing.

And right now Trent and Jaden were practicing together at the middle school, father and son working drills, calling plays, peas in a pod, looking like they belonged together.

Remorse made her sigh within, but she choked it back. Right here, right now, she had a job to do and intended to do her best, with or without Rocco's approval.

"What a night." Jaden grinned at her as things wound down later that evening. "Is it always this busy on weekends?"

Alyssa nodded. "Crazy, huh? How'd practice go today?"

"Great. Trent and Chris know everything. Did you know that Trent was a soldier?"

Oh, yeah. She knew. She hid her reaction behind an easy nod. "Yes."

"And that he served on two fronts? Iraq and Afghanistan?"

The thought of that danger scored her internally, but she had no business worrying about Trent at all, especially in aftermath. He was safe and sound here in Jamison, his presence providing a daily wake-up call to her conscience. "I didn't know all that."

Jaden ran his hand through his hair, a Trent gesture, the move endearing. "He said he'd show me pictures sometime."

"Great."

Jaden leaned forward, sensing her reticence. "Would that be okay?"

Alyssa drew a deep breath, shut a file drawer and headed toward the front dining room where the last diners relaxed over coffee and dessert. "It would be fine, honey. Trent's a good guy."

"He is." Jaden's agreement didn't surprise her. He'd always been astute, a willing pupil. Again, his father to a tee. She'd done all right, but nothing that notable, which had put another strike in the fatherly approval column. Was it odd that she'd rather be here, waiting tables and making food, than in a classroom learning geometric functions?

Obviously so. But she took quiet pleasure in her father's request for her to come back and help. That was a huge step for him. Of course Alyssa knew that while he didn't mind Rocco's gruff attitude contained in the kitchen, Gary would never allow such outbursts where the public might be privy to them. He kept the dining rooms, the grounds, the decorations pristine from season to season, regardless of how long or hard he had to work to do so.

He'd ingrained that same ethic in his daughter.

"Mom? Can I check out downstairs?"

Alyssa nodded. "Actually, I wanted to do some stuff down there myself while the guys and gals wrap things up here. You want to take me on in a game of pool?"

"Sweet." Jaden sent her a grin over his shoulder. "Are you ready to crash and burn?"

"Talk's cheap, kid. Let's see what you've got."

She beat him easily, grinned, tousled his hair and sent him home a short while later. He thought his reserves were endless, but she had no trouble noting the tiredness in his face as nine o'clock approached. "You've had a busy day. Go home. Sleep. Rest. I'll see you in the morning."

He stifled a yawn. "Grandma says we're going to church at ten."

Alyssa hemmed and hawed, then nodded. She'd begged off last week because of the move and Cory's illness, but now...

Fresh out of excuses. And it wasn't such a big deal, to spend an hour in the old church and pretend it mattered. That she belonged there. She knew better, but that was between her and God. "We'll be up and ready."

Jaden sent her a look that said too much. Knew too much. Then he nodded, hugged her and headed out the lower level. At the door he turned. "So no one uses this anymore?"

Alyssa surveyed what had been a popular spot when she was a kid. "Kids have games on their cell phones now. Or fancy game systems on fifty-two-inch TVs in their living rooms." She shrugged. "Rooms like this are obsolete."

"It's a shame we can't do something with it," Jaden went on, his look assessing. Like Trent, he was always thinking ahead, moving forward, his internal thrust engine constantly engaged. "Make it into something else. Especially with how pretty this is out here." He waved his hand to the terraced garden that led to the hillside setting.

His words sent Alyssa's thoughts tumbling in rapid fashion. As he ran down the hill toward home, a jigsaw puzzle of fit and form took shape in her brain. The white limo, the laughing bridal party, the sweep of terraced garden beneath the cedar-pillared floor-to-ceiling windows and doors. She turned slowly, appraising the room without the aging games and machines. She pictured the support pillars redressed in ivory stain, the walls repainted, new carpet, a dance floor right there…

She pointed, not caring that no one was around to see, the idea taking root, detail by detail.

The size of the room, it's accessibility to the patio garden outside, the terraced look, the curving steps. The southern exposure of The Edge offered great photo ops, the gardens work of Susan's hands, their tapered flow complementing the glass and cedar rise of the building above.

Alyssa could almost feel the ambiance, hear the music, see the couple dancing, heart to heart.

All right, that image went a little over the top for a realist like her, but from a business perspective and a feminine vantage point, The Edge could be transformed into "The Place" for weddings starting next season. Grabbing her notepad from her pocket, she jotted thoughts and plans as they came, filling pages of possibilities.

The trick would be approaching her father.

And the key to that would be convincing her mother first. While partners, Susan never went over Gary's head. But her mother wasn't afraid to press her points home, a strong business-woman in her own right.

Alyssa clapped the notebook shut and hurried upstairs to close things up. Her father might argue. He might get defensive because it wasn't his idea. But in the end, Gary Langley liked a good business proposition, a strong stance in the community, a leadership role. Alyssa's job was to convince him and Susan that her idea could help do just that.

Chapter Ten

"Trent."

Susan Langley didn't look very surprised to see him, but then she'd always been more in tune with people than her husband. If Gary was the brains of their family business, Susan was the soul. Trent inclined his head and nodded toward the living room, the television sounds announcing Gary's presence. "May I speak with you and Gary, please?"

Her face softened, but her eyes held warning. "Of course. Come in. Would you like coffee?"

He shook his head. Depending on Gary's wrath, this visit could be over in milliseconds, like a think-on-your-feet military exercise. This was real life, the human-drama kind, and he'd be willing to bet neither he nor Gary would enjoy the coming minutes. But since it had to be done, he might as well get on with it.

"In here." Susan led the way through the spacious kitchen, around the corner and into the family room beyond. "Gary. Trent's here."

Gary's jaw stiffened. He stared at the TV as if deciding whether to turn. Cory made his decision easy. "Twent!"

She barreled across the room and flew into his arms. "You came to see me!"

"I did." He couldn't help but match her grin with his, her

spontaneity contagious. "Thank you for playing with me today."

She nodded and squeezed his cheeks between two tiny hands, her inquiring look quite serious. "You wanna see my ni-ni?"

He matched her expression and nodded, solemn. "One of the reasons I came by."

She wriggled down, dashed across the room, grabbed a dusk-pink blanket that had seen better days and raced back to his side, offering it up for his inspection. "See? It's my very special ni-ni."

He stooped low, trying not to let Gary's negativity affect the little girl's enthusiasm. "I see that. And you're right—it is very special."

Susan leaned in. "As opposed to her just plain-old-special ni-ni."

Trent frowned, confused.

Susan jerked her head left. A second pink blanket lay along the back of a loveseat, its brighter tone attesting its lower status. "That one is for emergency use only. Like if this one can't be found. This," she dropped her gaze to the blanket he held, emphasizing the adjectives, "is the *very special* ni-ni."

"Lines of demarcation." Trent nodded and grinned. "I'm military enough to understand that. Well, here, young lady." He handed the very special blanket back to Cory. "Make sure nothing happens to that, okay?"

"'Kay."

Susan took her hand. "Cory and I are heading out back to check on the garden. I think it's almost dry enough to till up. We'll be back in a few minutes."

Gary didn't respond.

Susan shot Trent a look of sympathy mixed with concern before she led Cory outside. Trent moved around Gary's chair and took a seat opposite Alyssa's father.

His initial impression was that not much had changed. Gary still had that bulldog expression, chin jutted forward, a frown creasing his eyes, his attention riveted on a TV game show.

Looking closer, Trent noted his pallor, his breathing, discomfort keeping his breaths shallow.

Go easy.

He hunched forward, locked his hands together and said, "I've come to apologize."

"Too little, too late."

"I agree."

Silence stretched between them, a quiet standoff, a war of wills. Gary caved first. "I gave you a job."

"Yes."

"And worked around all your crazy football scheduling for over two years."

Not without a lot of grumbling and guilt-slinging, but Trent left that alone. "Yes."

"And how did you repay me? By running around behind my back. Getting my daughter pregnant. It was cowardly and deceitful."

"It was, which is why I'm here." Trent leaned forward, refusing to buckle under Gary's glare. "I was a kid. I made mistakes. Took liberties I shouldn't have because of my feelings for Lyssa. Regardless of my feelings for her it was a grievous mistake and I'm sorry."

Gary stared as if willing him to say the wrong thing, make the wrong move.

"But now that I know about Jaden, I need to fix things as best I can. I need to support him. Help take care of him. And that's awkward right now because he has no idea who I am."

"That won't last long around here."

Trent nodded agreement. "You're right. And I'd rather he hear it from us than from others, but Lyssa wants him to have a little time to get to know me. Soften the blow."

"It's hard to admit to your kid that you've lived a lie for twelve years."

Gary's scorn bothered Trent. He jumped to Lyssa's defense, then wondered why. "She thought she was doing the right thing."

"You buy that nonsense?" The older man raked him a look that said he'd lost ground.

Trent treaded with caution, considering Gary's health. "I think it fits Lyssa's personality. She's always sacrificing for others. And she's a little timid, but I think her heart was in the right place initially."

"And later? She could have told you eight years ago." Gary offered the argument point-blank, questioning Trent about Alyssa's motives. As if he had a clue. "Why didn't she?"

"I have no idea."

Hadn't he asked himself the same questions? He considered what Reverend Hannity said that morning, that circumstances sometimes inspire silence. He shrugged. "But what's done is done. I'm here to apologize and promise to take care of my son. Now that I'm aware, I'll take my responsibility seriously."

"See that you do. And keep your distance from my daughter."

The thrown gauntlet. Trent stood and sidestepped the emotional challenge. "That's impossible because we share a child. And Lyssa and I are adults now. Capable of making our own decisions."

"Not while she's living under my roof."

His arrogance made Trent want to run out and put a security deposit on an apartment for Lyssa, just to pull Gary's chain. But since his intentions toward Lyssa reflected Gary's stance, there was no earthly reason to argue the point.

Although he wanted to. And that realization concerned him.

He paused, thought about offering his hand, but recognized rejection when he saw it. He nodded Gary's way. "I'll see myself out."

No reply.

Not unexpected. And it could have gone worse. A lot worse. Maybe Gary's health issues had done something time hadn't. Calmed his temper, his exaggerated self-importance.

Over the years Trent had witnessed both sides of Lyssa's

father. The warm, sociable man who ran a good business with strong customer relations and a tough-but-fair attitude with his employees. Most of them anyway.

But his bullish traits appeared away from the job, in family settings. Probably part of the reason he'd gotten along with Rocco all these years, an old-world mentality that allowed for little gray in his black-and-white, right-and-wrong world.

Trent prayed he'd never be like that with his son, that while he was willing to take a father's stance of authority, he'd remain humble enough to see the whole picture.

He waved to Susan and Cory as he climbed into his car and started the engine. Dusk had fallen while he was inside, and as he turned the car around, the lights of The Edge glowed picturesque above him.

He stared up, imagining Lyssa at work, her dark hair clipped back, her gentle manner effusive when greeting customers, hugging children, setting tables. She provided a calm, inviting presence, her nature more Susan than Gary.

His thoughts moved to Jaden.

His son was working the family business from the ground up, pressed into service to see what it took to make a dollar, build a business. All good things.

A part of him wanted to skirt the lower part of the hill and weave the car up, go see them.

Him, he corrected himself. See him.

He didn't.

He cast one more glance to the pretty setting above, the outside lights bathing the layered garden and hill below, then turned his car toward Route 19 and the motel, promising himself he'd start looking for a place to live after church tomorrow. A yard to lay roots. Plant a garden.

A home of his own, the first one ever. And the fact that Jaden could share it with him, at least some of the time, made the opportunity that much sweeter.

Chapter Eleven

Sunday-morning traffic congestion in Jamison.

Who'd have even considered such a notion, Lyssa pondered as she wove the SUV into a tight parking space.

The historic idea of having five churches face forward around a circled median played logistical havoc with innocent churchgoers from ten until noon every Sabbath, even though the churches tried to cooperatively schedule services to avoid the hassle.

But with the advent of nice weather, no one was in much of a hurry to leave the village following services, so the best-laid plans went for naught, early gatherings impinging on later ones, with folks assembling in groups to chat and catch up.

The bagel shop set up an outdoor cart of fresh, warm kosher breads and sweet, sugar-topped muffins, the enticing aroma holding people longer yet.

Head down, Alyssa refused to make eye contact indiscriminately as she walked into Good Shepherd Church for the first time in over a decade. It was different at The Edge. There she was on her own turf, home ground.

Here? In God's house?

She felt like everyone was looking at her, noting Jaden and seeing Trent's face, hair and mannerisms in everything the boy did.

And when Trent walked in and took a seat in the pew opposite them, the noose of misgiving tightened.

How could people see them both and not know? Not assess? Not condemn?

Her heart sped up. Her fingers went numb. Her toes tingled. *Stop. You'll make yourself crazy. Calm down.*

Try as she might, she couldn't.

Her vision danced, the candle-lit altar splitting into two. She blinked hard, twice, but the split vision remained, a sure sign of a crushing headache.

Tiny notes sounded from the keyboard, dancing pings, one note at a time, the individual sounds a call to worship.

The congregation stood.

Alyssa followed suit, trying to make her knees behave, her heart calm.

No.

The notes continued, growing in warmth and speed, the hymn's sweet words encouraging God's people toward peace. Faith. Calm. Quiet.

How Alyssa wanted that. Longed for it. And many a night she begged God for it, the peace and quiet she'd known as a child, the harmony of a family that loved, a gift she'd taken for granted. Standing there, with Jaden by her side, her mother holding Cory, and Trent standing tall and broad opposite her, she felt as if the four corners of her life were rushing together, a sure collision with no means of escape.

But the warm invitation of the hymn's words, the call to silence, the urge to leave the chaos behind soothed her soul. Quieted her heart.

The song advised her to find peace. Be at peace.

The calm cadence filled her, tucking itself into holes she'd refused to acknowledge until now.

Jaden sent a look her way, his expression wondering.

She reached out and squeezed his hand, knowing she couldn't stop time from moving forward, but somehow not caring as much as she had moments before, the peace enrobing her, the choir's voices touching her profoundly.

Reverend Hannity smiled at her moments later, a look of welcome warmth, an invitation to come back often. Alyssa smiled back, feeling...

Refreshed.

Calmed.

Cared for.

And when he offered a gesture of peace and goodwill later in the service, advising the congregation to share that peace, Alyssa faced Trent across the aisle with more courage than she'd felt in a long time.

He offered his hand.

She took it. Raised her gaze.

"Peace be with you, Lyssa."

She felt people watching and tried not to care. "And with you."

Then he leaned beyond her with a big smile and shook Jaden's hand, so like his own. Then her mother's.

Cory reached out to him, imploring him to take her.

Trent hesitated.

Alyssa knew what would happen if he didn't. Cory might be a peaceable little thing, but she wasn't afraid to go after what she wanted. In the middle of a quiet church service, that wasn't necessarily a good thing.

Alyssa sighed and touched Trent's arm. "It's okay. You can hold her. She's taken a shine to you."

He smiled as Susan handed her off. "The feeling's mutual. Shall I stay here?"

His look swept their pew.

Talk about awkward.

And delightful.

The mix of feelings rushed back, erasing some of that earlier peace. Alyssa nodded and they moved in to make room for Trent.

The perfect family.

For a photo-op millisecond, that's how they appeared. Father, mother, two kids and a grandmother alongside, gathered together to worship en masse.

The reality smacked of unedited cable TV, but a tiny part of Alyssa wondered if the dream was possible. Plausible. Standing alongside Trent, seeing Cory cuddled in his strong arms, hearing his voice during the hymns and responses, she had a fleeting glimpse of happily ever after.

But she'd given up fantasyland long ago. Still, having Trent this close, the family image fresh and ingrained, she realized the time had come. They needed to tell Jaden the truth, open the doors to building his relationship with his father.

Sure, she was scared. Who wouldn't be? But she'd promised herself to stand strong. Honesty was a part of that pledge.

She'd talk to Trent outside. Let him set the time frame. They'd do it together and let the chips fall where they may, but then at least it would be done. One more confession purged from her soul. It wasn't enough, she realized, thoughts of that Montana cemetery shoving aside more of her fleeting peace. Not even close. But it was a beginning.

Too close.

Trent felt it the moment he accepted the child, her cuddled warmth thawing an edge of his toughened soldier heart. Soft blond curls tickled his cheek with her every movement.

She didn't stay with him long, but long enough to give him a taste of what life could be with a wife, a family, and long enough to bring home what Lyssa stole from him. Time with his son. His boy.

As he handed a squirming Cory back to Alyssa, he realized he was stuck there, in her pew. Next to her. He tried not to notice the sheen of her hair, the hint of auburn peeking through, coaxed out as he'd suspected it would be. The curve of her cheek, her ivory-washed skin looking as soft and sweet as he remembered. The brush of her arm against his, the quick, tentative look she shot his way, as if hoping he didn't think it intentional.

While a part of him wished it was.

That thought jump-started a surge of inner annoyance.

His songbook lay across the aisle, and there were no extras in Lyssa's pew. Crossing the aisle to regain his former seat or procure the book would cause more looks, more stares, more whispers.

Trent hated drama. He embraced practicality and usability, an engineer's stronghold, a soldier's manner.

But when Lyssa held open her songbook, her raised brow inviting him to share the page, the innocent invitation took heightened meaning, lodging somewhere inside his soul.

Her height made it easy to share the book. Her proximity made everything else difficult. Trent found it hard to stay grudging when the scent of freshly washed hair made him think of how that hair had slipped between his fingers. Having Alyssa's shoulder tucked against his arm reminded him of how easy it had been to tuck an arm around the woman beside him. Walk with her. Talk with her. Share his dreams, his plans, all of which had included her.

And then they'd gone too far. The proof of that stood nearby: a strong, handsome boy, solemn and kind.

From bad can come wondrous good.

Reverend Hannity's eyes met Trent's. The older man gave no indication of the connection, but Trent felt it to his toes, knowing their reckoning would soon be at hand and wondering how Jaden would handle it.

How Lyssa would handle it.

The hymn came to a lingering close, the notes fading like a late-day beam of light.

His hands paused on the book, his fingers brushing Alyssa's, that tiny connection frissoning awareness. But despite the gentle minister's gaze and the peaceful surroundings, Trent had no desire to be any more aware than he already was. Deliberate and cool, he removed his hand, kept his gaze locked on the altar and stood, rock-solid straight and tall, pretending it never happened.

Trent was a sensible man. Honest and forthright. While a part of him worked to understand a young girl's sacrificial choices, he couldn't imagine coming to terms with what held her silence the last eight years, once he'd been commissioned.

She should have told him. The fact that she didn't negated the tiny quirks of electricity now. He was a thirty-one-year-old man trained in self-sacrifice for the good of his country. Avoiding self-indulgent sparks wasn't all that big a deal.

Although it felt like one at the moment.

"Mommy, can Twent come for supper?"

"No."

Their collective responses made Trent wince. Cory's face darkened, not understanding why they were so quick to douse the flames of friendship when all the little kid wanted was to play with him. Trent bent low. "I've got some work to do this afternoon. A nice lady is coming by to help me look at houses."

"You don't have a house?" Cory's look of sympathy made him smile. Her next words erased that smile. "We don't either. Mommy says we might get one someday, but for wight now we'll make do, wight, Mommy?" She tugged on the hem of Alyssa's light sweater, the rolled hem saying the garment had seen hot dryers on a regular basis.

"We have a lovely house right now, with Grandma and Grandpa," Lyssa countered. "And we'll be moving into our very own apartment on Tuesday. That's plenty for us."

Cory digested that, then swung back toward Trent. "But you're buying a whole, big house?" Her voice squeaked up in question. "For just you?"

Her surprise made it seem a little indulgent, but Trent nodded. "I always wanted a house here. Now that I'm back it's a good time to shop."

"Then I can visit you!" Excitement heightened Cory's tone, drawing attention from others who'd gathered outside, enjoying the softness of the day and the communal spirit. "Oh, I will like that so much, Twent! Can I visit you in your new house today?"

"Not today, sugarplum." Lyssa shook her head, her voice firm while all Trent wanted to do was make the little girl happy. Obviously he had a bit to learn about fatherhood. Or Cory was fairly adept at being the most adorable, approachable little kid he'd ever met. Not that he knew many, so that assessment might be less than accurate. In any case…

"Trent doesn't even have his house yet. Buying a house takes a long, long time."

While she was right, Trent saw her ruse for what it was, buying time without losing the little girl's favor. And Lyssa's move made perfect sense. Ease the child away from a growing relationship with him. He'd be a steady presence in Jaden's life, but it was in Cory's best interests not to get too attached, right?

So why did he bend down again, clasp the child's hand, meet her gaze and say, "You can come visit after I move in, okay? And maybe we can play together. Or get ice cream."

"I love ice cream this much." Cory's outthrust arms magnified her words. "And not just banilla either. I like so many kinds."

"Vanilla." Lyssa skipped right over Trent's invitation and went right to enunciation. "Put your top teeth against your lip and make it shiver, just a little."

"Va-va-va…banilla."

Lyssa smiled. "Good try. Keep practicing. We'll get it."

She stood, clutched Cory's hand and made it a point not to meet Trent's gaze. "We've got to go. I'm working tonight."

"Jaden, too?"

She shook her head, looking anywhere but at him.

"Then maybe he and I can get in a practice once I'm done house shopping."

She hesitated, torn. He saw it in her stance, her expression, the tight jaw. Then her gaze settled on the white church, the thin spire arrowing through the trees. A softness touched her profiled features. She paused a moment, then nodded, still not looking at him. "Sure. Give him a call. Or nab him away from those guys right now and check it out. Since I'll be working it would be nice for him to be with you. And Trent..."

He dipped his head, waiting.

"You're right. We need to tell him."

Fear and joy mingled within him, but outwardly he simply nodded. "Today?"

"You've got stuff going on today and I have to work. Tomorrow? In the evening? He's got school until three, and then we're moving stuff into the apartment. We can do it there or—"

"Here."

She glanced around, frowning.

"With Reverend Hannity. He was a big help to me growing up."

Alyssa weighed that, shrugged and nodded, looking cornered but resigned. "You'll set it up?"

"Yes."

"Okay."

Susan approached from the bagel stand, a glossed white bag in one hand. "Shall we get these home to Dad while they're still warm?"

"Of course." Lyssa smiled at her and headed for the back parking lot, Cory's hand in hers. The child balked. Lyssa leaned down, her gaze intent, then nodded and scooped the little girl up, cuddling her against her shoulder. Cory's yawn surprised Trent. It was just a little past eleven. Did kids get tired that quickly?

From the shy, tired smile she gave him over her mother's shoulder, he guessed so. Watching Lyssa's retreat, he realized that Cory's pale cheeks weren't like her mothers. Lyssa's light skin glowed with health. Cory's appeared dull in comparison. And shadows rimmed her big blue eyes.

She'd been sick, he knew that, but glancing around at the other children in the village green, none of them seemed to share that washed-out expression.

Fear niggled him.

He suppressed it to avoid being an annoying childless thirty-something who thought they know everything about raising a child with no practical experience. He shut down the nudge of concern, bought a half dozen bagels, checked with Jaden about a late-day practice on the green, then headed home to meet the real estate agent in more comfortable clothes.

By tomorrow night Jaden would know Trent was his father. How would the boy handle it?

A host of possible scenarios swept him, making Trent question their judgment. Were they doing the right thing? Was the status quo so bad?

For the moment, no. But since his relationship to Jaden was obvious to many, it was time to come forward and begin a new chapter in their lives. With a strong mother and father, Jaden would be fine. Just fine.

And while Trent was certain they'd made the right decision, he wasn't afraid to put it in God's hands, praying for strength. Openness. Honesty.

And forgiveness.

Chapter Twelve

"You bought a house this quick?" Jeff Brennan asked the next morning, sending a look of mock disdain to Trent's convenience store coffee cup and holding out his more upscale variety. "And you drink that stuff?"

Trent sipped and nodded. "Two dollars cheaper than that half-milk thing you're sporting and I didn't actually buy the house yet. I put in an offer in. We'll see if they accept it." He quirked a brow. "Did you need me, Jeff? Because one of us has work to do."

Jeff grinned. "That would be you. I get to shadow you while studying the intricacies of creating tight-and-trim contract bids."

"Great."

Jeff settled into a chair, looking way too comfortable. "And I get paid to do it."

"Only if you learn something."

Helen's voice straightened Jeff's slouch in a heartbeat. "Yes, Grandma."

Trent laughed and handed Helen the current bid folder. "Let me know if you see anything that needs adjusting. These are preliminaries for the new two-way radios that meet current army specs. Similar to what you've done before but with advanced channel potential to screen signal detection."

"We can handle this?" Helen's expression said she trusted his response.

"With a full night shift, yes, which almost doubles your employee load because we're increasing the B shift to match the daytime staff."

"That's a lot of people," Helen countered. "And a hefty responsibility if things go bad."

"You lose one hundred percent of the chances you never take." Trent met her look of question with one of confidence. "You have the facility, the know-how, the in and the opportunity. Carpe diem."

"Seize the day." Helen accepted the folder and gave a brisk nod. "You're right, of course. And this is the very chance we've been hoping for."

She turned to leave, then paused with an over-the-shoulder look at Jeff. "Learn something."

"Yes, ma'am."

She smiled. "That's better. And call your mother. She worries about you."

"I'm thirty-three."

"Nevertheless."

"Will do." Jeff flashed her a grin and resettled into his chair, but without the casual attitude he'd been sporting earlier.

Trent noted that with a glance. "Much better, silver spoon."

"A negligible point since she makes me work as hard, if not harder, than everyone else."

"Good."

"It is," Jeff agreed. "My father's interest in the company went down the tubes with his drug use…"

Trent frowned. Helen's son-in-law had taken his family on a rough ride for a lot of years, including embezzling company funds to support his illicit habit. A rough road for a good, upstanding family.

"And while my mom is a great person, she didn't inherit Grandma's thick skin which gave him greater opportunity because he played on her soft heart time and again. And her faith." He shrugged. "Luckily, I got an extra dose of the rough-tough Walker genes. So what happens if we lose this first bid?"

"We continue bidding. I don't lose easily or often. And I know my stuff. We're in a good spot because of our track record with the military."

"But those contracts were small potatoes compared to this." Jeff waved a hand toward Trent's desk, where neat piles attested his gathered information.

"True, but that's how the military works. They try you out, get a feel for your stability and follow through. And if we miss the boat with this first bid, I'll be right there at the head of the line with the next."

"Good. So where's this house?"

"On McCallister Street."

"In Jamison?"

Trent nodded, settled into his chair and set his cup down. "Close to everything. I love it."

"I figured you'd grab something more upscale, one of those posh places lining Route 19. Or over on West State. Brooklyn Avenue. They're more affordable now, too, with people having to sell when the economy tanked."

The elegant Wellsville neighborhoods Jeff cited were note-worthy and executive-friendly. Trent recognized that. And he knew some people were comfortable making a killing at some-one else's expense. He wasn't one of them. And Jeff might not understand Trent's need for the old-fashioned village setting, the hometown feeling he craved. Trent wasn't sure he understood it himself, but he'd known the moment he walked in the front door of 132 McCallister that he'd come home. "I like the village. If the weather's bad, there's nothing I can't walk to. Except work."

Jeff nodded. Wellsville was about fifteen minutes south of Jamison.

"It's peaceful. Quiet," Trent added.

"It folds up the sidewalks at seven o'clock."

"Only nine months of the year." Jeff's expression said that was nine months too long.

Trent smiled and shrugged, remembering what the people of Jamison had done for him. "I love that town." The phone rang, interrupting his moment. "Trent Michaels."

"Julie and Keith just accepted your offer on their home." Mary Kay Hammond sounded excited for good reason. "No counteroffer, no strings, no contingencies. Talk about a sweet deal, Trent."

He laughed, delighted, but teased, "That just makes me wonder why, Mary Kay. What horrible surprise did we overlook?"

"Not a thing," she declared firmly. "That's why we're making it contingent on a clean engineer's inspection. I'll set that right up, and since they've already moved into their smaller home in Allegany Station, we should be able to close this deal ASAP."

"Perfect."

Some would think using his years of savings to pay cash for the house a foolish idea, but Trent liked things paid for. He wasn't big on owing anyone anything, and his lifestyle suited him.

It also put him in the sweet position of being able to pay cash for the historic two-story colonial with the sprawling yard, a tire swing, and shade trees that invited boys to climb high into the upper reaches while cooling the old place from the midsummer sun. A creek that ran along the lower back, feeding a broad fishpond with fresh water.

The house said home in every way possible, from the wide front porch to the rustic cranberry door that set off the tawny gold exterior, the look finished by multihued hanging baskets.

"What do you need from me next?"

"Not a thing," she told him, keyboard keys tapping lightly as she spoke. "I'll have this all set pending the engineer's inspection. I've set that up for Friday morning, and we could close as early as next week. Or the week after."

"Seriously?"

"Absolutely. I haven't had a clean deal like this in the last eighteen months, so I should feel guilty about taking my commission."

"Better yet."

She laughed out loud. "Operative term being 'should.' Since I don't, I'll take my commission and remember this fondly the next time I have to walk someone through reams of government paperwork to keep Fannie Mae happy."

"Sounds fair to me." Trent jotted Friday's inspection on his calendar. "I'll meet you and the inspector Friday at ten."

"I'll bring coffee."

Trent grinned. "Doughnuts wouldn't be a bad idea. Considering the ease of the deal, I think it's the least you can do."

"I'll stop by Dunkin' before I head up Route 19. Spoil you a little."

"After all those years in the Army, I'm not sure how to handle being spoiled."

She laughed. "Well, if this venture of yours with Walker Electronics works magic like Helen hopes it will, I won't be the only one spoiling you."

Her words humbled him.

What if the whole thing went sour? How disappointed would these folks be if the sought-after contracts never materialized?

But they would, he assured himself. Trent took nothing for granted, part of the reason he'd attained commanding status in the Army at a young age. He wasn't afraid of measured risk, as long as he had major control of the variables, like in this case. Still, nothing was firm with the government until signed in triplicate and stamped Approved. And just in case this first bid fell short of the goal, he and Jeff would have the next one ready to roll.

Alyssa pulled up to Good Shepherd on Monday night much like she had the previous morning, heart racing, totally revved despite employing every calming maneuver she'd ever learned.

Jaden glanced around, curious, then followed her example and climbed out of the car. "Why are we here?"

Because I've been living a lie with you for twelve years and never told you what a good and wonderful man your father was. Just let you believe he couldn't take care of us.

Um… No.

"We're going to meet with Reverend Hannity."

"About church stuff?" Jaden sounded more resigned than thrilled, fairly typical for his age.

Trent's greeting saved her from answering. "Hey, guys." He stepped out of the reverend's back door, dressed in a casual knit shirt that looked new and comfortable, an unattainable luxury on Alyssa's budget, and khakis that didn't look wrinkled from sitting.

Alyssa tried to tuck the frayed strap of her purse farther down her arm, and wished she'd taken time to buff up her leather slip-ons.

"Trent. Hey." Jaden stuck out a hand, grinning up at Trent as if hoping the night was about to morph into an impromptu football practice.

Trent matched the grin, like father, like son. "Hey yourself. You work on that shift-right, left-lateral pattern?"

"Yes, sir."

"That's my boy."

Alyssa cocked her head at the phrase, pleased and concerned. For Jaden to find out about his father meant she had to confess to being a dishonest mother. And while her initial rationale had made sense to a seventeen-year-old pregnant girl, her later reasoning was nothing she'd be sharing with Jaden, not now. Not ever. Or Trent either, despite his obvious curiosity and anger.

But he didn't look angry tonight. He looked…

Nervous. And eager. Kind of like Jaden used to look on Christmas Eve, wondering if Santa would come. Expectant but cautious, never getting hopes up too high.

"Come in, come in!" Pamela Hannity swung the door wide behind Trent and stepped back, her hand out in welcome. "I've got cookies on the reverend's desk, go on in and help yourself to a seat. He'll be right there."

"Thank you, Mrs. Hannity." Alyssa met the older woman's warm, friendly gaze and tried to maintain her composure when every nerve inside was pushing her to turn tail and run.

"Look at you, you dear thing!" Pamela exclaimed, accepting Alyssa's hand and then giving her a little spin. "More beautiful now than when you left, isn't she, Trent?"

Umm…awkward.

"And how happy your mother is to have you back, with your dad's problems and all," Mrs. Hannity continued. "You," she placed her hands on Alyssa's shoulders, her affectionate gaze not nearly as innocuous as she pretended to be, "are a gift from God."

Her gentle words helped.

Alyssa hadn't felt like a gift from God in a long time, but something in Mrs. Hannity's voice inspired a spark of worth within Lyssa's heart, lighting a minute corner of the soul she thought she lost. "Thank you."

Her whispered reply softened the older woman's gaze, her look of wisdom offering feminine understanding. "You're welcome, child."

Benediction. Acceptance. Forbearance. They emanated from the pastor's wife like lotion on wind-chapped skin, emollient and smooth.

She bustled them into the reverend's office, a midsized room that was more like a small living room. Easy. Comfortable. Inviting. His desk sat tucked in a corner, almost an afterthought, while the chairs and sofa invited repose.

"Mother's shown you in, I see." The reverend hurried into the room, his hair disheveled, his cotton shirt twisted. He straightened himself the best he could, sank into a chair and wiped a cloth across his forehead. "I haven't played soccer like that in nearly thirty years. It felt good." He smiled up at Mrs. Hannity, sipped the water she brought him and relaxed into his chair before mopping his brow again. "This is why children come to the young." He nodded Alyssa and Trent's way, his gaze sweeping Jaden. "Because we grandparents wear out more quickly."

Trent followed the thread. "Although if you're too young, people make mistakes." The gaze he rested on Alyssa wasn't accusatory this time. More like...understanding. Empathetic.

Alyssa swallowed hard and turned Jaden's way, refusing to drag things out. "Jaden, a long time ago I told you that your father couldn't be with us, couldn't care for us."

He nodded, looking suddenly trapped, an uh-oh expression darkening his features.

"That was true those first years, but the real truth was, he didn't know about you."

Jaden frowned.

"I never told him I was pregnant."

The frown deepened. "Why?"

Trent laid a hand on Jaden's arm. "Because I was going to West Point and they have rules there about marriage and children. Your mother knew if she told me that I'd want to marry her, and raise you and she didn't want me to give up my dream of being an officer in the army. Getting a great education. She thought it was the right thing to do at the time."

"So that means—"

"That I'm your dad." Trent kept it simple and straightforward, true to form. "And while I'm sorry to have missed the first years of your life, I'd love to be a part of them from this point forward."

Jaden's stricken expression reflected his inner turmoil. He turned Alyssa's way. "You lied to me."

She had but hated to admit it. "Yes."

"Why?"

"First for Trent, so he could get through school." Alyssa bit her lip, shifted her gaze outward and stared at the small oak and maple grove beyond the window, the baby leaves curling out and up. "Then later I was afraid to tell the truth. Afraid that Trent would be angry and disappointed in me. And afraid that he would think I was after something once he was done with school and had a promising career ahead of him."

"You never told him?"

Alyssa shook her head. "No."

Jaden shifted his attention to Trent. "And you never suspected?"

"No." Trent weighed the question, then shook his head more firmly. "Not at all. I just figured I'd disappointed your mother by my actions and she was understandably ready to be done with me. When I saw you last week…" he angled his head and shrugged, his hand indicating Jaden, then himself "…it was fairly obvious."

Jaden stood, visibly upset. "To you maybe. Is this why you've been playing football with me? Getting buddy-buddy?"

Trent's sharp eyes said one thing as he assessed Jaden's posture, his indignation. His relaxed body language said something else. "I wanted to get to know you. Have you get to know me before springing this on you."

Jaden swung Alyssa's way. "Do you ever stop lying?"

Alyssa paled.

Trent frowned. "Jaden—"

Jaden turned his way. "No. You don't know what it's like, never knowing what's real, what isn't. What's honest, what isn't. Having your mother make excuses for everything, every step of the way." He turned back toward Alyssa again. "I just want someone or something to believe in, Mom. Somebody that's strong enough to be honest. To tell the truth."

His words road-mapped Alyssa's life. She'd hedged the truth in so many little ways, that lying to protect him and Cory became natural. And downright sinful. She averted her eyes and nodded. "You're right, Jay. I should have been honest with you once you were old enough to understand. And I should have told Trent about you a long time ago." She drew a deep breath, blinked back tears and raised her gaze. "Can you forgive me? Start fresh?"

"I don't know." The impudent look Jaden shot at Alyssa heightened Trent's concern. "I don't know how to believe you."

"Step by step."

They all turned, the pastor's voice surprising them. He swept them a glance and splayed his hands, palms up. "You take it step by step from this day forward. Learn to be honest, even when it hurts," he directed his gaze to Alyssa, then shifted to Trent. "Learn to forgive, even when it hurts." Now his look moved to Jaden, standing between them. "And we learn to accept our parents' failings, just like they accept ours. Just like God accepts ours."

Jaden's face darkened. He obviously wasn't quite ready to accept what had been thrown at him. He paused, then straightened his shoulders and headed for the door. "I'm walking home."

Alyssa started to stand.

Trent restrained her with a hand to her arm and a shake of his head. "He needs time. He'll be fine."

"But—"

Trent shook his head again, understanding the boy before him much like he did the one within. "Let's give him some space to sort things out."

It was plain she wanted to follow the boy. Reassure him. And just as obvious that Jaden didn't want her to.

Trent's heart heaved within his chest. He didn't know how to comfort Jaden and was mad that he wanted to comfort Alyssa, her face pale and stark, their son's rejection and accusations hitting their mark.

The reverend reached out a hand to each of them as Jaden stormed out the back door. "Father, bring peace to this family. Unite them as You united that holy family in Bethlehem, as You united the women beneath the cross, as You united those left in turmoil following Christ's crucifixion. Bless this young couple, Lord, and lead them in Your ways. Your path. Your hope."

Young couple?

Trent shoved that notion aside, the thought of his son's anguish tormenting him. Alyssa's posture said she felt the angst and condemnation, the almost-physical struggle within him. Despite the pastor's gentle hands joining them in prayer, she'd shrunk into her seat, as far from him as possible under the circumstances.

Pray for her.

The gentle words of conscience prickled Trent's emotions.

Remember what you read, what you discovered, what she's been through. Pray for her.

Right now praying for Alyssa ranked about dead last on his to-do list. Seeing Jaden's disappointment, his anger, the sense of betrayal…

A fierce blanket of protection surged forth, wanting to cover his son, remove the trouble and worry from his heart and soul. Isn't that what fathers did? They protected? Nurtured? Guided? Led?

And he'd been denied all of this because Alyssa had pulled a duck-and-cover mode.

Words failed him as Jaden's disappointment stirred too many memories of his own childhood, that sense of not belonging, of not being loved by those who should love you most: your parents.

Trent stood. "I have to go."

The pastor looked like he wanted to say something, then stopped himself. "I'll be praying for you." He nodded Alyssa's way. "For both of you. All of you."

Trent didn't dare respond. He left, his jumbled thoughts intermixed, entwined. He needed to get away, walk, run…

Think.

Pray.

He put the car into gear, shifted and headed down the road toward Route 19, thoughts of Alyssa's face and Jaden's anger warring for sympathy and attention. If only…

No. He refused to go there. He knew better than that. There were no ifs, ands or buts. The Army had taught him to assess and act, not dwell on past performance. He needed to pull those skills to the forefront and focus on them.

Jaden needed time.

All right, then. He'd give him the space he needed and remain a steady presence in his life, letting Jaden set the time frame. Days, weeks, months… Now that he knew he had a father, he'd come to realize that Trent was in for the long haul.

And Alyssa?

A part of him prayed she'd be fine with all of this, that she'd emerge stronger, more capable, braver than she'd been in the past. Another part realized he was a big part of the reason she'd gone into hiding. Misguided or not, her preservation of his dream was nothing to be scoffed at or taken lightly. In football terms, she'd taken one for the team, and despite his resentment of what she'd cost him, the team leader inside him saw her actions as brave, though foolhardy. Often as not, that's what heroes were made of. Brave, foolhardy sorts that walked where angels fear to tread.

And while he couldn't possibly agree with her choice, he understood it. That in itself was more than a little scary.

Chapter Thirteen

Alyssa studied her sketch pad, then shifted her gaze to the lanky boy below, watching her son struggle with life's turns and twists, knowing she bore responsibility for way too many of them and hoping she'd finally taken a right turn.

Please, God. Let this be a right turn. A step forward.

The tiny prayer fostered in her heart, her soul. Now that Jaden knew the score, she'd come clean on one level and the relief that offered was notable. Sure, she'd been dealing with the stubborn anger of an adolescent for nearly a week, but he'd seemed more accepting the past few days.

She saw Cory dash out of her parents' house and infiltrate her brother's practice zone. From the rear level of The Edge, Alyssa couldn't hear the conversation, but from the way Jaden seized his little sister, spun her in the air, tucked her under his arm and ran with her, she was pretty sure Cory had just become a replacement football.

Her father crossed the yard at a slower pace, a newspaper tucked under his left arm, a mug balanced in his right hand. He looked calmer today. More peaceful. Rested.

A ruckus from the restaurant's primary level grabbed Alyssa's attention. She slapped the sketch pad shut and hurried upstairs, the tone of Rocco's voice adding speed to her steps and stress to a tumultuous week that seemed to stretch on forever.

"What's wrong?" Alyssa moved across the dining room floor, surprised to see Rocco near the restaurant entrance, his profile intimidating, his features dark with anger.

A customer faced him, a man dwarfed by Rocco's size but standing his ground nonetheless.

"You no like the steak, you no eat here again."

Rocco's words added fire to Alyssa's feet. She moved between the two men, laid a gentle hand on the customer's arm, drew his attention from the daunting cook and asked, "What's going on? Can I help you?"

"Getting this behemoth out of my face would be a great start."

For you and me both, thought Alyssa. She nodded and turned toward Rocco. "I've got this."

He pulled upright, squared his shoulders and faced Alyssa squarely. "You no have nothing. You go play while there is work to be done. If you do your job, this…" he waved a hand toward the irate customer and the college-aged waitress hovering nearby "…no happens. Why you no do your job so I can do mine?"

Insolent. Insubordinate. Impudent. Disrespectful.

Yup. That about summed it up. And Rocco would never think of coming out of the kitchen, facing a customer, if Gary was around. He knew Gary's fastidiousness, and the golden rule of food presentation: The customer is always right.

"I said I've got this." The possibility of repercussions caused by Rocco's tirade magnified her courage. Dissing customers didn't happen at The Edge. Ever. And the thought that Rocco's tantrum might cost future business gave her the guts to stand up to him. "I'll see you in the kitchen when I'm done."

His face darkened, anger at her summary dismissal caricaturing his features.

A quiet voice interrupted from just behind her. "You okay, Lyssa?"

Trent.

She had no idea where he'd come from or when he'd taken a position behind her, but his presence offered welcome support for her stance between the angry men. She nodded, keeping her gaze trained on Rocco. "Fine, but thanks for asking. Rocco was just going back to the kitchen."

Rocco swept them a look of disgust, whipped his apron off and threw it across the entry, making his exit as grandiose and melodramatic as he possibly could, muttering terse phrases in Italian.

Taking a breath, she turned back to the customer and extended her hand. "I'm so sorry about that. Please, tell me, what was the problem?"

The man shook his head, shrugged and raised his hands, palms out. "What does it matter now? Our meal's cold, my wife's upset and the baby woke up so there's no hope of either of us eating at this point."

Alyssa scanned the room, spotted a woman feeding a baby, and said, "Do you have a little time?"

The man shrugged again, then nodded. "Well… Yes. Some."

Alyssa walked him back to the table. "We've got two options. I can warm this up, I'll feed the baby and you guys can relax and enjoy your meal or…"

She flashed them both a smile of humor-tinged apology. "You can make my day by feeding your baby while I step into the kitchen and fix your meals the way you want them. Jocelyn has your order, right?" She nodded toward the waitress who looked equally relieved to have Rocco back in the kitchen where he belonged.

Jocelyn raised a hand. "I do."

Alyssa cleared the plates on their table and inclined her head toward the baby. "A beautiful boy. How old is he?"

"Four months."

"So sweet." She made eye contact with the baby's mother and winked. "You feed him. Let me work some magic in the kitchen."

"Does your magic include a transfusion of nice genes into your cook?"

Alyssa sent the man a look of understanding. "I'll take care of it, sir." She handed the plates to Jocelyn and stretched out a hand to the customer. "I'm Alyssa Langley. My parents own The Edge. Dad recently had open-heart surgery and he'd be mortified to know what happened."

That statement had the calming effect she'd hoped for. The man nodded and shrugged. "I've got a business of my own, actually. Having good help isn't easy these days."

Alyssa gave him a commiserative smile and headed for the kitchen. "I'll be back in a little bit. Jocelyn will make sure you're comfortable while I redo this."

As she rounded the partitioned corner and headed toward the swinging door to the kitchen, Trent fell into step alongside her. "I'm coming with you."

Alyssa tried to brush off his concern. "Not necessary."

"It is." He pushed open the door, allowed her to enter, then followed, his gaze sweeping the wide kitchen. "I see not a thing has changed."

It hadn't, but Alyssa hadn't realized the import of that until Trent said the words. In the last dozen years the world had changed for various reasons, economic, catastrophic and acts of terrorism painting a whole new global world.

The Edge hadn't kept up. While in some ways that was good because trendy food often went out of vogue quickly, in others it meant they weren't striving to meet the individual needs of their customers. Amazing how one short statement opened her eyes to part of the current trouble.

Trent grabbed an apron from the bin inside the door. "You do the main dish. I'll do the sides."

Rocco scowled.

Alyssa ignored him, pulled two porterhouse steaks out of the cooler, rubbed them with her father's freshly ground blend of herbs and spices, then put them on the wood-fired grill to sear.

Jim stepped around them, slid a tray of twice-baked potatoes into the warmer, nodded to Trent and stuck out a hand. "You probably don't remember me…"

Trent grinned and grabbed the offered hand. "Jim Pearson, you played running back for Hornell."

"Yeah, man." Jim's smile said Trent's memory impressed him. "While you ran circles around us. How're you doing?"

Trent slid his gaze to the two fresh plates he held in the other hand. "Right now trying to placate an unhappy customer."

Rocco stiffened but kept his silence. Obviously big, strong guys didn't get the same kind of rude, obnoxious behavior he bestowed on women.

Jim didn't miss a beat. "Gotta keep the customers happy. Too much competition out there to mess this up and I've got a wife and a kid. Paychecks are a good thing."

"You got that right," Trent agreed. He set the plates onto the warming rack, dropped an order of fries into the hot oil and checked the warming drawer for foil-wrapped baked potatoes while he watched Alyssa grill the steaks to perfection.

"Done."

"They look beautiful."

She acknowledged that with a shrug. "We'll see. Sometimes a customer's perception of medium-rare doesn't match the cook's."

If her attempt at peacemaking appeased Rocco, he didn't show it.

Trent added a baked potato to one plate with a side of sour cream and butter, then piled seasoned steak fries on the other. "I'll follow with the vegetable medley."

"Thanks."

Alyssa refused to think of how nice it was to have him in the kitchen with her, to have someone watch her back while Rocco fumed. She'd pledged to stand on her own two feet, but she couldn't deny the layer of strength and protection Trent's presence offered, even temporarily. They dropped off the freshly prepared food, stood by while the couple tasted their steaks before nodding approval, cooed over the now-happy baby in his monkey-motif car seat, then stepped away.

"Well."

"Well." Alyssa laughed at the mimicked speech, glanced down, then brought her gaze back up to his. "Thank you."

His gaze softened. A spark of awareness flashed, a hint of heat that transported her back to another time. Another place.

Meeting his gaze, she wondered if his thoughts had gone in the same direction, to teenagers in love, laughing, talking, sharing every secret dream and goal.

"My table's waiting." Trent jerked his head right.

Alyssa turned.

A beautiful young woman sat at the table, her profile to them, busily texting someone very important, no doubt, while Alyssa cleaned plates, mashed potatoes and waited on tables.

Well, there was no competing with that. Not like she was trying to anyway, right? She turned back, determined to hide the nip of jealousy dogging her heels, and saw a different look in Trent's eye. Knowing. Assessing. And more than a little amused.

He leaned close. Real close. Close enough that she could guess the thread count in his well-cut wool sport coat, feel the warmth of his breath against her cheek and smell the mix of Drakkar, peppermint and just a hint of French fry oil. "Business meeting. Sales rep for a company that produces made-to-order motherboards. I didn't even notice she was runway gorgeous. Really."

"Didn't ask and don't care," Alyssa retorted.

Her blush said otherwise. Trent's little smirk of agreement matched the almost unnoticeable clench of his left cheek muscle, a little move that said he was trying not to laugh but wanted her to know he was trying not to laugh.

That brought back a flood of memories, too, of Trent drawing her out of a young girl's funk every time she felt like she let Gary down. The unspoken way he had of making her laugh at herself, sort things through. That appreciation became the cornerstone for her later choices. For heading out west, keeping her pregnancy secret. For one quick moment, she wondered again what life would have been like if she'd just owned up. Would it be like Trent had intimated? They'd have gotten married, he'd have gone to school somewhere else, and she could have had the last twelve years filled with love, warmth, and security?

At that moment she realized the import of what she gave up based on a teenager's quest to do the right thing.

Shadowed memories clouded her brain.

Trent moved closer, his eyes concerned, his voice a whisper. A wonderfully husky whisper. "No going backward, remember? We said we'd move forward from now on. Take care of Jaden. Feel our way, step by step."

She nodded and moved back, easing proximity that was wreaking havoc with her insides.

The blonde at the table turned.

Alyssa moved farther back yet.

The blonde might be a sales rep, but Alyssa read the look of interest in pretty brown eyes outlined in perfect makeup, not too much, not too little.

Um, yeah, about that? She hadn't graced a makeup counter in too many years to remember, not even for free giveaways. That would have required gas to get back and forth, and wasting money like that didn't cut it, not when there was Jaden to care for, followed by her roller-coaster years with Vaughn.

But she'd read somewhere that overuse of makeup aged skin texture, so being broke might actually land in the plus column. Eventually.

Trent looked like he wanted to say more.

She didn't give him the chance. "Thanks again for the help."

She started to move away when his voice stopped her. "Not that I'm counting, but I do believe that's the second rescue in less than two weeks."

That voice.

Was she imagining the warmth? The teasing? The hint of something precious and long-lost?

Her self-protection mode clicked into high gear because no way in this world could she handle treading water with Trent

Michaels. The teenaged Alyssa had discovered that the hard way. The grown-up version had a lot more at stake. Two kids, one of which she shared with the good-looking former soldier standing behind her.

She turned, cool and deliberate. "Since neither intervention was really necessary, they don't qualify as real rescues."

He quirked the first full-fledged Trent grin she'd seen since running into him nearly three weeks back. "Oh, they qualify, all right. I'm trained in rescue missions, young lady, by the best of the best." He flexed an arm muscle that didn't need flexing to show his strength, his military-trim physique. He cut a great figure even in a suit, and Alyssa knew firsthand that he didn't need to pad his shoulders to heighten the impression of big enough, strong enough, smart enough to take anything on. "We Army boys know a good rescue when we see it."

Endearing.

That's what he was being right now.

Sweet and endearing. And she couldn't afford either, so she shifted an eyebrow up, sent him a look of disbelief, turned on her heels and walked away, wishing she didn't have to. Wishing...

Nope. Not going there.

She was strong and growing stronger. She'd faced Rocco and emerged victorious. And she'd have done it with or without Trent's help, she was sure. The fact that his help felt so good gave her cause for concern.

But she'd walked away, like she knew she should. And that helped solidify the ground beneath her feet.

Chapter Fourteen

"Are you the only person in town making cakes for this gig?" Alyssa swept her mother a look of disbelief that encompassed the spotless kitchen behind her. "I don't even want to know how late you were up last night."

"Late enough." Susan stacked three boxed cakes and headed toward the SUV. "I figured since Dad and I can't help with the rebuilding of the youth center, the least we can do is feed people."

"A small island nation, minimal."

"I heard that."

"Good." Alyssa laughed, following her mother outside. "You were supposed to."

"Trent picked Jaden up this morning?"

"Right on time." Trent had asked Jaden to help on the opening weekend of the project and Jaden had agreed, almost eager. As if he coveted time with his newfound father now that he'd grown accustomed to the idea.

"And you're okay working down there?"

Alyssa frowned, confused.

"With Trent there?"

"Oh. Um..."

"Gotcha," Susan replied, her expression knowing.

"Mom."

"Enough said. Go. The sun's going to melt the frosting if you don't get the air going in this car."

Alyssa leaned down and gave her mother a kiss on the cheek. "And you don't mind having Cory?"

"Like you'd be any help down there with her running around. She's fine here. She'll amuse your dad and that in turn amuses me."

Alyssa laughed. "But he's doing much better now, and not nearly as grumpy."

"Old bear." Susan made a mock scowl, tinged with affection as Alyssa climbed into the driver's seat. "I'll see you later. Maybe I'll bring Cory down for a playground visit later on."

"She'd love that."

The refurbishing committee had orchestrated traffic, parking, food and steady access to all the churches. A coffee/breakfast bar was set up to the north, lunch would be served from the back of Holy Name on the south side of the circle, Ginger Baxter's church. The youth center had been an old church building set in the rear center of the circle. When their congregation had grown, they'd moved that building back along the road heading east and built a new brick-and-clapboard church up front, although new was a relative term for a church that had been there nearly forty years.

A middle-aged man in an orange reflective vest stopped Alyssa's progress as she entered the circled green. "Breakfast, lunch, dinner or cleanup?"

"Lunch. Dessert, actually." Since she had to cover the shift at The Edge that night, she'd have to leave mid-afternoon. "I just need to be able to get my car out by two-thirty or so. Have to work tonight."

"Head behind Holy Name," he instructed, looking very official and serious despite the bright orange vest in the morning summer sun, a look that might have been a little over-the-top for Jamison. "The left section will be clear for people needing to get in and out."

"Gotcha."

Alyssa smiled her thanks, followed his directions and breathed a sigh of relief once she had the SUV parked. Ginger Baxter's voice greeted her as she closed the driver's door. "You made it through the parking police, I see."

Alyssa laughed. "It wasn't easy, I assure you. There are those among us—" she tipped her thumb toward the road "—who take their job quite seriously."

"But you got to park in the special section," Ginger noted, teasing. "Did you bat your eyes or flash him that pretty smile?"

"Neither, which is kind of sad, don't you think?" Alyssa flashed her a grin as she opened the back of the car. "I just pleaded my working-girl status and he let me in."

"You're working tonight after all this?" Ginger waved a hand to the organized chaos surrounding the green.

"Well, you've got three kids, a house and a preacher husband, and you're like twenty-months pregnant, so I think you're actually one up on me. I just have to run a restaurant."

Ginger raised the corner of the first box and sighed in gratitude. "Your mother's lemon cream cake." She swiped a finger to a spot of frosting on the lower edge of the cardboard circle inside, tasted the sweet/tart lemon frosting and sighed. "I could eat this whole thing right now."

"To go with the chocolate pies you've been eyeing?" A nice-looking man approached from the side, not too tall, his manner confident, self-assured and more than a little amused. "Give me those before you trip and fall and we spend the day at the hospital instead of here."

"At this point the hospital sounds mighty good," Ginger shot back. She relinquished the boxes, grabbed two more, then motioned toward Alyssa. "This is Alyssa Langley, Gary and Susan's daughter. Alyssa, my husband, Tom, the second pastor in my life."

Tom stretched out a hand, balancing his two cakes in one very capable arm, nodding recognition. "Jaden's mom."

"Yes."

He grinned, approving. "Great kid. Trent's got him up on the roof, doing tear-off."

"He… What?"

Ginger's expression noted Alyssa's surprise with an uh-oh look, but Tom brushed it off. "Best time to learn roofing is when you're young enough to fear nothing."

"Don't mothers have a say in this?" Alyssa turned, scanning the rec center area, but the majority of it was obscured by the newer church in front.

"Mothers get to pray. A lot."

"Except Mary Kay," Tom noted, laughing. "She's right up there with the boys, tool belt and all."

"And holding her own," Ginger agreed. "Whereas I—" She dropped a belabored look to her midsection.

Tom leaned in, his gaze warm, his tone tender. "You're keeping yourself quite busy growing our child." He laid his free hand against her swollen belly, and Alyssa fought the well of emotion within.

She'd never had that, not with any of her pregnancies. Trent had been left out, Vaughn had been pretty much a nonentity with her pregnancy for Cory, and then…

She tried to block the flood of images from the ill-fated pregnancy that followed. Vaughn's anger. His deliberate blows.

"You all right?" Tom leaned her way, concern darkening his eyes.

Alyssa straightened, squared her shoulders and nodded but added astute to Tom's list of qualities. "Fine, thanks."

He opened the door for them, but his look said he wasn't buying it. Alyssa avoided further discussion by heading outside once the cakes were in the cooler.

A soft breeze ruffled her hair as she rounded the corner of the centered brick church, the cool shade a comfort compared to the glaring sun on the roof of the north side of the rec center. The south side was shaded by thick, tall oaks but the north side didn't share that luxury.

She noted her boys straight off, not like it was hard to do.

Boy, she corrected herself firmly. *Jaden's yours. Trent isn't.*

But what a pair they made, working side by side, shoulder to shoulder, prying old tiles loose and tossing them to the Dumpsters below. A sheen of sweat brightened their faces, identical blue sweatbands circling their brows, short, dark curls above. Jaden's longer hair left curls below as well, whereas Trent's buzz left his neck open to sunburn and black flies, an annoyance these first warm weeks. Alyssa wondered if he'd thought to apply sunscreen and bug spray there, then caught herself.

Not your concern.

The fact that she was concerned was bothersome.

"Alyssa?"

She turned, recognizing the voice. "Megan?"

The other young woman laughed, running forward to clasp her hands before dropping them to hug her. "I can't believe how long it's been!" Megan Russo stepped back, eyed Alyssa, then nodded. "And you're still beautiful. Brat."

Alyssa laughed. "You, too. Amazing how twelve years has made so little difference, right?"

"Twelve years." Megan leaned in, her voice going deep and serious. "Do you know how old that makes us?"

Alyssa nodded. "Older than our mothers were when you and I first met."

"And that's just wrong on more levels than I care to consider," Megan went on. "You here to help or ogle Trent?"

"Trent who?"

"Uh-uh." Megan grabbed her arm, turned and scanned the roof. "Stake your claim early, girlfriend, because after today every available woman under forty will have put him on the cookie-baking list."

"Trent's more a grill-a-steak kind of guy, so we should be okay." Alyssa sent her a bemused look. "And because I'm not interested, the issue becomes moot."

"You may not be, but he sure is."

Alyssa followed Megan's gaze.

Her eyes locked with Trent's, and even from this distance

it was easy to see that Megan was more right than wrong. Her heart drummed an absurd rhythm in her chest. Try as she might, she couldn't break her gaze from his, those gentle eyes watching from above. Then Jaden asked Trent a question, interrupting the moment. Father turned to son, nodding. Then he bent down, mouth moving, a shingle rake in his hands. She saw Jaden nod in understanding, turn the bar, then nod again.

The scene she witnessed gripped Alyssa's gut.

She'd cost them both so much. Time. Love. Companionship. And at too huge a cost to even begin to make things right.

Megan seemed to sense her shift in mood, but that was understandable. They'd been friends a long time before Alyssa had pulled her disappearing act. She tugged Alyssa's arm. "Come help me set up the breakfast foods and we'll snag some coffee. You can catch me up."

Alyssa nodded, not daring to look up again, Trent's gaze unsettling. On top of that her beautiful son was shoveling tiles off a rooftop, and managing the job quite handily, which meant he was growing up way too fast, another hurdle she didn't need to face at eight in the morning.

Coffee sounded good. And girl-talk with Megan. Neither one would put her in the dangerous position of resisting Trent's inviting strength.

"Did you make this?" The warm voice in the vicinity of her left ear sent a tremor along Alyssa's neck, the appreciative whisper raising goose bumps along the top of her arms. "Cold?" Trent asked with a raised brow, as if he already knew the answer.

"Just fine, thanks, and no, I didn't make it." Alyssa poured glasses of lemonade for the workers on lunch break and kept her gaze from meeting his. "Mom did. Taste good?"

"Perfect. I love carrot cake with cream cheese frosting. I actually had it for the first time in the Army." He licked his fork appreciatively and sighed disappointment that the cake was gone. "It's been an ongoing love affair ever since."

"Would you like another piece?" A part of her wanted to move him down the line, but a bigger part longed for him to stay right there, talk with her. Tease her. Maybe…

Do. Not. Go. There.

He scanned the number of people with obvious regret. "Naw, that would be greedy. Did I tell you I'm closing on Julie and Keith Wasserman's house next week?"

The tray of full glasses left her temporarily out of diversionary tactics. She chanced a glance up, realized it was probably not a good idea to meet Trent's gaze when he looked so wonderfully sun-rumpled and handsome, despite the grubby clothes and bits of roofing dotting his hair. Not obeying the inner caution that warned her to resist, she reached up and brushed debris from the back of his hair, away from the food and drinks. "You're a mess."

Her touch brought a smile to his eyes. "But I clean up nice."

There was no denying that. "You do." Obviously a change of subject was in order. "Their house is on McCallister, right? The big gold colonial?"

"With the red shutters and window boxes. Yup. It was love at first sight."

"First the cake, now the house." Alyssa smiled a welcome and nodded toward the tray of drinks as a couple of guys coated in drywall dust approached. Obviously the inside crew.

Trent leaned a smidge closer. "Old habits die hard it seems."

Her breath caught. She knew what he meant, exactly what he meant. They used to laugh about falling in love right off, knowing the world would scoff at a pair of teens who believed such nonsense. But Trent's tone of voice said it might not have been all that ridiculous.

And yet it was, so she patently ignored the hint of enticement. He stepped back as if sensing her quandary, but not minding nearly as much as she did. "I'll see you later when I drop Jay off."

Alyssa nodded, purposely not prolonging the conversation by saying she was working. He'd figure that out when he got to the house. Prolonging her time with him didn't bode well for either of them. The heightened interest in his eyes pushed her to tread slowly. She'd had to bare her soul on some important issues already. She had no intention of making it a clean sweep, airing her linens for the world to see. If that meant putting Trent off, so be it. He'd be more than put off once he understood the kind of girl she really was, and she'd had enough stress to last a lifetime. No reason to compound it by deliberately placing herself in line for more heartbreak. Been there, done that, obviously not a quick learner in affairs of the heart. But this time she was in charge, and about time, too.

"Hey, Trent, the guys want to throw the football around the back field until it's time to get back to work." Jaden grabbed a lemonade, wolfed it down and had Alyssa refill it in record time. "Thanks, Mom. So, what do you think? You got time to throw around with us?"

Noting Lyssa's constructed look of indifference, Trent figured Jay's timing was perfect. He'd planted a seed of interest, and half hated himself for doing it, but couldn't resist. Which was what got them into trouble in the first place. Being twelve years older, he should have smartened up some. Older equates wiser, right?

And yet…

He wasn't any wiser. Not around her.

Proximity to Lyssa was a minefield equation. He'd had enough of those during battle. Finally back home, he just wanted peace. Quiet. Normalcy.

He nodded to Jay, tossed his plate and cup into the trash and trotted off with his son to play a little touch football, hoping that running beneath the hot sun would take his mind off how pretty she looked in her ultra-flattering lace-trimmed top. He knew he wasn't the only one who noticed how alluring she looked because he'd caught two different guys sending admiring glances her way.

And while he had no claim to her, he recognized the gut-clench feelings those looks inspired and realized he was in deep water. The urge to hold her, laugh with her and protect her grabbed him by the throat and it was all he could do not to stake a claim with an embrace that said "Hands off, she's taken, look elsewhere."

Because he had no business doing that, he backed off physically, but made eye contact with both other men, his frank stare cooling their jets for the moment. That maneuver would only last so long. Sooner or later some guy would sweep her off her feet, realize what a wonderful person she was, marry her and have a host of babies to join Cory and Jaden.

Yeah, like that was going to happen.

The distinct possibility put a burr between his shoulder blades that made him run faster and throw stronger. When the return-to-work whistle called an end to their makeshift game, Tom Baxter laughed and clapped him on the back, the older man catching his breath. "You run that fast all the time or just after pretty girls give you the brush-off?"

"You saw that?" Trent scowled, mopped his brow with a towel and then lobbed the towel at the laughing reverend. "Can't a guy crash and burn in private?"

"Not in Jamison."

He got that right. "True enough. Doesn't matter anyway. She's not interested in rekindling old fires, which is for the best, I suppose."

Tom's gaze swept the area where Lyssa helped the other ladies with cleanup and shrugged disagreement. "Oh, she's interested all right. She hasn't taken her eyes off you all morning. Just running scared."

His words paused Trent. He stopped and turned, realizing the reverend was right. "But why?"

"Now that's a question only the lady can answer." Tom made a face. "And being a woman it could be any one of a hundred things, but in general when a lady doesn't let herself relax and enjoy the life God's given her, it's because she's mantled a truckload of guilt around her shoulders."

Guilt?

Trent eyed Lyssa curiously. "I'm no stranger to that one myself."

"Men are different," Tom told him. "They rationalize their behaviors, accept them and move on."

Trent frowned, recognizing the truth in Tom's words.

"Women absorb their guilt, bear it on their shoulders and can't let it go. In their heads they think they should be held to a higher standard. When they mess that up, guilt reigns."

His words made sense to Trent. Hadn't Reverend Hannity said much the same thing? That Alyssa might have regrets dogging her heels?

Thoughtful, he nodded to Tom and trotted back to the rec center area to help load shingles onto the conveyor belt, trying to shove aside thoughts of Lyssa. He spent the remainder of the afternoon on his knees with a nail gun, the repetitive pops pushing thoughts of romance and guilt out of sight, out of mind.

Mostly.

Chapter Fifteen

"Jaden?"

The boy's head popped up from the far side of the roof. "Yeah?"

Alyssa pointed to her watch. "I've got to head out so I can get to work. Your dad will bring you home, okay?"

Saying the words in public nearly choked her, but it wasn't as if anyone on the green or the roof hadn't either heard or figured things out, so why be coy?

Trent's head appeared to Jaden's left, brow drawn. "You're working tonight? You've been here all day."

"And your point?"

His frown deepened. "You're the closer?"

"Of course."

"But—" Concern deepened his frown, his features.

Alyssa tapped her watch again. "Gotta go. Thanks for bringing him home."

She headed for her car, hoping the morning command post had kept their promise of not blocking the exits for her parking area. She didn't have time to hunt down car owners, not if she wanted to grab a quick shower and look presentable. As she ducked beneath the spreading limbs of a hard maple outside Holy Name, she nearly plowed into Miss Dinsmore, her tenth-grade science teacher. The aging woman put out a steadying hand to catch a tree limb.

"Miss Dinsmore, I'm so sorry! I didn't see you coming through there."

"You were eyeing the ground, lost in thought," the older woman agreed. "Hard to see what lies in front of us when our focus lies elsewhere."

Typical Miss Dinsmore, saying so much with so little. Alyssa smiled. "True enough. You're just arriving?"

Miss Dinsmore nodded. "I had review classes at the high school today. The regents exams are just around the corner and success often hinges on proper preparation."

"In so many things."

"Yes." Miss Dinsmore gave her a gentle smile, her eyes frank but easy. "Now while subject matter and retention weren't your forte in school…"

Alyssa couldn't argue the assessment. Math and science weren't exactly a cakewalk for her. Trent had been a big help on those her junior and senior years.

"Application of concepts was right up your alley. And that's a skill that can't be taught, my dear." She tilted her head, looking wise and gracious. "Lots of people have the brains to memorize, but few have the ability to apply those concepts to everyday life."

Her words caught Alyssa's full attention. "I was good at that?"

"Exceptional. You're a born facilitator, a person who can see the overview and plan for it while delegating responsibility."

Miss Dinsmore didn't compliment lightly. Ever. Her words nudged Alyssa's self-esteem up a notch. "Thank you, Miss Dinsmore."

"You're welcome, but I expect you need to get off to whatever's got you in such a hurry on a beautiful Saturday afternoon."

"The Edge."

"Ah." Miss Dinsmore smiled. "Your father's lucky to have you back."

Alyssa sincerely hoped so. She stretched out a hand. "Make sure you grab some of Mom's cake before it's all gone."

"Which one did she make?"

Alyssa laughed out loud. "Most of them."

"That's your mother."

"Yes." She smiled proudly.

They headed in opposite directions, but the aging woman's words stuck with Alyssa. Miss Dinsmore had always believed in her abilities and capabilities, even as a kid. She'd shrugged off Alyssa's challenges in school and prioritized her strengths. Seeing her, knowing she still carried the same fire for today's students, made everything seem better than it had before.

Which was ridiculous, right? Why would one person make such a difference in the whole scheme of things?

The story of the little boy and the starfish came to mind, the child walking the shore, tossing stranded fish back into the sea, an endless task but meaningful to each one he saved.

"If you cannot feed one hundred people, feed just one." She'd taped that quote from Mother Teresa on her bedroom wall in Montana, a reminder that little things add up. Somewhere along the way she'd forgotten that, but seeing Miss Dinsmore brought it to mind. She headed home and then to The Edge, hoping to work on her wedding business proposal for her father once things slowed that night.

"Busy night?"

Jim gave a bemused shrug as Trent approached the back door of The Edge. "Cranking. And Rocco being Rocco let everyone know that working with an incompetent woman slowed things down and interrupted the flow in the kitchen."

"Jerk."

"That's for sure. Once he left at eight, things were smooth as silk," Jim added.

"Makes for a rough dinner hour, though."

"You can say that again. Jay's not here."

Trent paused a beat. "I know."

"Ah." Jim's expression stayed calm but knowing. "So you're here for Alyssa."

Trent ground his jaw, then shrugged. "So it would seem."

Jim laughed. "Well, good luck with that, old man. My wife will eat this up. She loves happy endings."

"Women."

"Yeah." Jim nodded but dropped him a wink. "Women."

Trent entered through the scuffed-up back door. The cooking area was ready for closing except for a few kettles and pans stacked by the dishwasher. He crossed through the kitchen, down the short hall and entered the middle dining room where the hall teed to offer access in three directions, making things easier for servers.

Cat Morrow saw him first. "Trent, hey. You looking for Alyssa?"

Was he wearing her name stamped across his forehead? Probably so, despite his earlier determination to keep his distance. So far, that wasn't exactly working as planned. "Yes."

Cat pointed toward the back staircase. "Downstairs."

"Really?"

She nodded and Trent headed for the stairway, wondering. The downstairs level of The Edge had been a teen gathering spot, but as game systems became minimized and more graphic-friendly, arcade rooms like this became obsolete. He walked down the carpeted stairs, saw Alyssa bent over paperwork at a decent-sized table and paused, studying her.

She should be tired after her long day. Exhausted. Trent knew what a busy Saturday night at a restaurant took out of you; he'd worked there for years, keeping pace with the constant ebb and flow of table after table for hours on end.

But Alyssa didn't look tired. Or harassed. Or disheveled. She looked invigorated, her eyes trained on the work in front of her, her gaze expectant as she jotted things in a notebook. Realizing she had no idea he was there, he cleared his throat.

She jumped, startled.

"Just me."

His words didn't have the effect he'd expected after being shut down earlier that day. The tiny flash of expectation when she jumped up made him think she might be almost happy to see him.

Almost.

He moved forward as she shielded the papers on the table, blocking them. He slanted her a grin and an upcast brow and peeked around her, letting her know she couldn't hide something in plain sight. Her height meant he had to get reasonably close to see the papers. So he did.

Normally she smelled like sun-ripened fruit. Peaches. Mangoes. Strawberries. The scented soaps a fruit basket of invitation.

Tonight she smelled of kitchen food and he didn't care a whit, the chance to be close to her outweighing everything else. She reached out a hand to shuffle papers aside and he caught it in his.

She stopped. Went totally still. Her breathing hiked up, as if his touch, his grip was ramping her heart the way it accelerated his.

One beat. Then two.

She started to lean back, a question on her lips, but there was only one question he wanted answered right then. So he leaned in to discern the answer, his mouth finding hers, wonderfully familiar, like coming home to a well-banked fire on a cold winter's night.

He didn't want to pause or shift his mouth because then she'd have the chance to tell him why this was wrong, why it wouldn't work, could never work, and for just that moment he wanted to believe what the little boy inside had believed. That somewhere, somehow a family waited for him, a place to call home. And he longed for that to be here in Jamison, with her. With their son. And Cory, that optimistic little breath of sweetness and light.

But he had to stop eventually or suffer on-the-spot cardiac arrest, so when he raised his mouth, he sighed, laid his forehead against hers and just held on for dear life. "Lyssa."

"Hmm?"

He smiled, recognizing that tone, the tiny whisper, glad she'd been caught in the moment, too, a part of him wanting more moments like this, a host of them, day after day. Night after night.

She pulled back, bit her lower lip in consternation, and tilted her gaze up. "Well."

"Yeah. Well."

She stepped back, her face going politely still, a look she'd polished in her years away. "I—"

"What's this?" He reached behind her as if the kiss never happened, or maybe as if it was the most natural thing in the world and needed no discussion. He raised the sketch pad, studied the drawing and then the room surrounding them. "A banquet room?"

She wrinkled her nose as if caught making mischief, which they'd been doing to a certain degree after all. That thought made him smile. He slanted his look down, approving. "This is brilliant."

"You think?"

"I know." He released her, stepped back, turned in a slow circle, glancing from the pad to the current layout. "And not hugely expensive."

"Exactly." She nodded, pleased with his endorsement, and that took him back to the younger Alyssa, feeling like she chronically disappointed Gary in some way or another, so anxious to please. "The bathroom and ceiling upgrades will be the priciest part but doable. And with the way Dad goes over-the-top with Christmas lights and decorations, we could host all kinds of holiday parties and balls on top of wedding receptions and fundraising events. Think of what that could mean to my parents' income. Instead of five months of diminished activity, they'd have three."

"Huge difference."

"Yes, if he'll go for it."

"You haven't shown him this?" Trent raised the pad.

Her hesitation hinted insecurity, but her words came out

strong. "Soon. I wanted to have all the facts and figures, so I've priced out the upgrades, the refurbishing, the local loan situation and state tax write-offs and incentives for Empire Zone initiatives."

"Smart."

She flushed, disbelieving. "Hardly. This is like drawing a straight line with a ruler. Step by step. But I think it's feasible, don't you?"

"Absolutely." He met her gaze and held it, realizing he'd defused her objections to the kiss by moving on, but a big part of him wanted one more reminder of what he'd lost so long ago.

Her look of uncertainty brought to mind Tom Baxter's words of wisdom. Alyssa felt unworthy. Always had. Trent knew it was bunk, but that didn't matter because she didn't believe it, not in her heart, and certainly not in her soul. And while part of him wanted to chase the shadows from those pretty hazel eyes, another part shied back from too much too soon.

Although it didn't feel too soon. It felt like he'd been in a holding pattern for a dozen years, just waiting for this time, this place, this moment, this woman.

Cat's voice brought him back to current-day reality.

"Lyssa? We're set up here."

"Okay. Thanks, Cat." She gathered her paperwork and headed up the stairs, the sound of the front door clicking shut announcing Cat's departure.

Trent followed, thinking wonderful things about women in black trousers and slippery floral shirts, remembering the feel of the soft, silky fabric beneath the pads of his fingers.

She turned at the top. "Did you need to see me? About Jay?"

He leaned against a pillar and let a lazy smile embrace her. "Just needed to see you."

"Trent…" She frowned, turned and walked to the front door, testing the lock. "This isn't a good idea."

"Best idea I've had in a long time."

"I'm serious, Trent."

"So am I."

She shut down the front bank of lights, walked past him toward the kitchen and hit the central switch, plunging them into darkness broken by two small lights that allowed them to make their way down the hall and through the kitchen. As she stepped out the back door, she tilted her head up, eyeing the stars, the sweet curve of her neck more mature than he remembered but just as lovely. "Gorgeous night."

"I'll say." His gaze wasn't directed at the stars.

She shot him a wary look and headed for her car. "Why did you come?"

"To make sure you got home safe."

His words surprised and pleased her. He saw it in her smile, her eyes. "Really?"

He followed her to her car, opened the door, watched her climb in and then closed the door, taking care not to jar her. He leaned down, expectant. She hesitated, then rolled down the window.

Halfway.

He grinned. "Really. It's late, it's dark, it's—"

"Jamison." Doubt skewered her tone.

He acknowledged that with a shrug. "Things happen everywhere. I'd just as soon they don't happen to you."

"Trent…"

He backed off and waved. "See you tomorrow."

She frowned.

"Church."

"Ah."

"And I'm working with Jay in the afternoon." He smiled. "See you then."

She started the car, thrust it into gear and headed around the building slowly. Creatures of the night loved to travel the grounds of The Edge after sunset, and they'd seen deer of all sizes feasting on fresh grass and the occasional landscaping bush, much to her father's chagrin every spring.

She saw nothing tonight but the headlights behind her, well back, Trent's presence a silent message of care. Safety. Such a little thing to make her feel so good.

Of course that kiss was nothing to be scoffed at or taken lightly and could bear a certain amount of responsibility for the sweet feelings assailing her right now.

He'd smelled…wonderful. Marvelous. A blend of wintergreen and Drakkar, with a hint of spiced soap thrown in, an enticing combination of guy scents. And while he held her, she felt like she'd come home at last, his arms, his mouth, his scent familiar, so incredibly dear.

But reality reminded her that despite what she felt emotionally and physically, she wasn't the same and neither was he. Trent had gone on to make something of himself, rising from nothing to a position of respect and intelligence. She'd done nothing more grand than pile mistake on mistake, a broken road of bad choices compounding one another.

He had no idea, and that was okay with Alyssa. She felt bad enough about who she'd been, what she'd done, and she was singularly okay with keeping the whole mess under wraps. She'd made it through, she'd made it out, and the new road ahead lay fresh.

Trent was a stand-up guy, interested in the girl he'd known long ago, not the woman she was now. She recognized that, but part of her wished the girl was still available because kissing Trent had been as near to perfect as she could imagine. Which only made it harder to back-burner the memory, the emotion, his touch and warmth drawing up so many reasons to move forward. But forward really meant backward, and no way, no how did Alyssa have the courage to come clean. Not even for Trent Michaels. Especially not for Trent Michaels. She wasn't strong enough to witness the look of disappointment in his eyes, or read the lack of respect.

At this rate, she was pretty sure she'd never be strong enough.

Chapter Sixteen

"There's no sense arguing," Susan scolded, turning the SUV into the church parking lot on Sunday morning. "I'm running shift tonight and tomorrow. Dad's much better and you need a break. On top of that, Cory Sue needs more time with you."

"You're sure?" Alyssa paused, her hand on the door handle, giving her mother a chance to back out yet hoping she wouldn't.

"Alyssa." Susan braced both hands on the front seat, leaned in and met her daughter's eye, her expression feigning distress. "I've been with your father night and day for four weeks now. Think about that a minute."

Alyssa didn't need a minute. "I was wondering," she admitted, grinning as Cory worked to unbuckle her belts. "But you seemed so stoic. So strong."

"Even the strongest woman needs a break now and again."

"Running a restaurant is taking a break?"

"You know your father better than most. A heart patient who's got a cold on top of it. What do you think?"

Alyssa inclined her head. "I think it's perfect. I've got some ideas I want to share with Dad, so maybe I can butter him up tonight."

"On his diet? Lotsa luck. He's feeling mighty deprived these days. And catching this cold just made him crankier."

Alyssa nodded toward Cory while Jaden headed for the stairs. "I'll sic Cory on him. He caves instantly."

"It's hard not to." Susan settled an easy look on her grand-daughter. "She's such a funny little peanut."

"I'm not a peanut, Gwammy. I'm a girl."

"Of course you are, dear." Susan bit back a grin and palmed Cory's head. "Peanut just means little. Come here, your nose is running. Here's a tissue."

"But I'm not little," Cory insisted, indignation hiking her protest, the unused tissue clutched in one hand. "I'm big. I wear big-girl panties now. See?"

Alyssa prevented Cory from displaying her princess under-wear to the entire parking lot by picking her up and smoothing a hand across her bottom, tucking in the folds of the dress. "We don't show people our underwear, remember?"

"Oops." Cory planted two tiny hands across her mouth, brows up, an "Oh!" expression painting her features. "I forgot, Mommy. Can I just *tell* them about my undies?"

A smattering of giggles broke out around them.

Alyssa shook her head and leaned closer. "No. Undies are private. And wipe your nose, please."

Cory nodded sagely. "Okay."

"Come here, sugarplum." Trent's hands grasped the little girl from over Alyssa's head, thrilling the girl and surprising Alyssa with his proximity. He balanced Cory on his hip for a moment and nodded toward the playground in the park beyond. "If you're really good in church…"

Cory nodded, eyes round.

"And listen to your mommy…"

Her gaze flashed to Alyssa and back to Trent with another nod of anticipation.

"Then I will take you to the playground after church and buy you ice cream later."

She grasped his cheeks between tiny, intent hands. "I wuv ice cweam, Twent."

"I know you do, sugarplum, which is exactly why I sweetened

the deal." He leaned forward and bumped foreheads with her. "You'll be good?"

Her head bobbed, earnest, the blond curls bouncing. "Weally, weally good."

"Okay." He handed her back to Alyssa and winked when she sent him a look of gratitude. "I'll be watching."

"'Cause you'll sit with us, 'kay?" Cory glanced from Alyssa to Trent as if it were a given. "Like you did before, wight?"

Susan leaned into Alyssa's side, her voice none too soft. "Did you pay her to do that?"

"Mom."

Trent grinned but was too much of a gentleman to give her a hard time.

A blush warming her cheeks, Alyssa headed into the church, wishing she could just be that girl whom he'd fallen in love with twelve years before.

Couldn't, shouldn't, wouldn't.

End of story.

Alyssa watched as her father crossed the backyard that afternoon, a glass of tea in one hand, a trowel in the other. She asked, "You're up to gardening?"

"I'm sneaking it in while your mother's gone. She won't let me do squat when she's around."

"Which is her way of saying she loves you."

"And unafraid to drive me crazy," her father attested. He knelt alongside a circular garden surrounding a colonial-style lamppost. "I want to get rid of the bulb debris and plant these marigolds."

He sounded reasonable and comfortable, making this a good time to approach him about some changes at The Edge. "I'll get rid of the old stuff while you plant the new."

"Good. Cory sleeping?"

Alyssa frowned and nodded. "Yes. She seemed exhausted this afternoon, didn't she?"

"Yup. Coming down with something again?"

"It seems so, but why? We just got her healthy."

"Kids do, though. Nothing to fret over. Probably just caught this stupid cold from me."

"I suppose." She leaned forward and tugged some insistent dandelion weeds from around the lamp's base. "But I'd like her to have a little more recovery time in between, you know? Jay didn't get sick like this, back to back."

"Different time. Different kid. It happens."

"I guess. If she's still not well Monday, I'm going to take her to the clinic."

"They've got that after-hours thing now, don't they?" Gary asked. "So you don't have to wait?"

Thinking of the cost of urgent care, Alyssa bit her lip but kept her head down. "In Wellsville. You know, you're right. I'll take her after she wakes up. Maybe a round of antibiotics will put her right."

Alyssa was just about to launch into the topic of the banquet room when Trent's car pulled up the drive. Jaden burst out of the passenger side, frantically waving, while Trent climbed more leisurely from his side. He spotted her across the yard first thing, the intensity in his eyes belying his easy stance. Her father glanced up, took in the situation and heaved a practiced sigh.

Alyssa shot him a look. "You're supposed to be planting."

"I've got eyes, don't I? You know what you're doing?"

"I'm not doing anything." She leaned forward, keeping her voice a whisper. "And I'm thirty years old."

He huffed.

Jaden came alongside, his exhilaration palpable. Alyssa straightened. Trent reached out a hand. She caught it and he helped her up, smiling when her knees creaked. "Ouch."

She scorched him with a look that only deepened his grin. "What's up, Jay?"

"I met Tom Hewitt."

"Say what?" Alyssa looked from Trent to Jaden and back again, unable to believe that the former Forty-Niners' great had wandered into Jamison. "How? Where?"

"Wellsville." Jaden was fairly bubbling with excitement. "He was in town for some promo thing and Trent introduced us."

"You know Tom Hewitt? The greatest wide receiver to ever play the game? Invited to the Pro-Bowl thirteen times and winner of three Super Bowls? *That* Tom Hewitt?"

Trent looked impressed by her knowledge. "The very one." He shrugged, pretending nonchalance. "The NFL is big on getting players to the troops, both here and overseas. We hooked up a while back."

Alyssa nodded Jaden's way as her father stood, ignoring Trent's offered hand with a grunt. "Jaden's been a Niners fan from the time he could walk. His DVD showed all the Super Bowl wins."

"He fades back, sidesteps left, spots Hewitt in the end zone and lofts the ball…. Touchdown!" Jaden threw his hands into the air and raced around the yard, looking a decade younger than his age before ending the run with a well-executed cartwheel. "My dad knows Tom Hewitt!"

Trent shrugged. "We're not exactly buds, Jay. But I know him, yes. And he's a great guy with one of the most intensive and respectable training regimens known in modern-day sports. You want to be good at this game?" Trent raised the football higher. "Be the best of the best?" He jerked his chin toward the ball. "Practice like a Niner."

"I will." Jay nodded earnestly, his expression a mix of joy and promise, a look that aged him before Alyssa's eyes. "I'm not afraid of hard work."

Trent smiled. "That's my boy." He switched his gaze to Gary. "You look better."

"I'm doing all right."

Alyssa cringed at the curt tone, but Trent ignored it. "Good to see. Jay, you want to work more or are you ready to call it a day?"

"More."

Alyssa staved their plans momentarily by raising her dirty hands in the air. "Jay, can you go get your sister up, please? She's been down a while and I don't want to have to wash up before I'm done here, but I want her awake enough to run to After Hours in Wellsville."

"Sure." He trotted toward the garage apartment, light on his feet, then hurdled a wheelbarrow in his path like it was nothing. Alyssa knelt again and sidled a look up to Trent.

"You made his day, you know."

"Lucky circumstance. Tom was nearby and didn't mind coming into town to hang with us. We bought him lunch at the Texas Hot and created quite the sensation." He frowned. "So Cory's not feeling well? Again?"

Alyssa gave him a knowing look over her shoulder. "Another cold. Or something. She's just not herself." She grimaced concern, then shrugged. "And Tom was nearby? Trent, we're in one of the most remote areas of New York. Nothing's nearby."

He grinned. "Most days that's not a bad thing. Kind of a nice little hideout down here, tucked at the edge of the mountains. Our own Brigadoon."

Brigadoon. The fictional village that sprang to life once every hundred years, a fantasyland of peace, hope and laughter. Alyssa would love to be tucked into a nook-and-cranny Celtic cottage in Brigadoon, beckoning candles lighting windows at dusk. For a fleeting moment she could almost feel and hear it, strains of mountain strings and fairy whistles floating on the breeze.

"Mom!"

Jaden's urgent tone jerked her back to the present. She stood and turned, swiping her hands across her thighs. "What?"

"Something's wrong!"

Wrong?

Cory.

Alyssa flew across the grass, Trent pounding behind her. Jay held open the door and she raced up the garage stairs and into the bedroom she shared with Cory. The sight of her dusk-tinged little girl stopped her, the girl's labored breathing the only sound.

Then Alyssa darted forward, grasping Cory to her chest. "Cory? Cory!" She turned toward Trent. "Call—"

His raised cell phone said he'd anticipated the request. Alyssa half heard his directives, but her attention was centered on the lethargic, fevered child in her arms. Holding Cory, feeling her struggle for air, helplessness resurged. Once again Alyssa felt besieged by things beyond her control with no idea how to help.

"We're sending her to Rochester." The young woman met Alyssa's fearful look with a straightforward gaze, pulling no punches. "Cory's got a heart problem we're not equipped to deal with here. They've got pediatric cardiologists at Strong Memorial. She'll be in good hands there."

"A heart problem?" Alyssa raised a fist to her mouth. She looked scared to death, and no wonder. Trent had felt a physical blow to his gut when he saw Cory in distress like that. How much worse her mother must feel.

The doctor's look assessed Alyssa. She frowned. "Undiagnosed, I'm guessing?"

Alyssa paled further. "Yes."

A look of understanding flashed in the doctor's eyes before she tapped the clipboard awaiting Lyssa's signature. "We've notified Mercy Flight. The transport team will be right in to prep her."

Fear marked Alyssa's and Jaden's features. Trent stood alongside, helpless, an unusual feeling for a take-charge Army captain. He caught the doctor's eye and tipped his head toward Alyssa. "She'll fly with her?"

"Not enough room. Sorry." She shifted her look to Alyssa. "Can someone drive you guys up? It's about a two-hour trip."

"I'll drive," Trent assured her grimly, his battlefield stoicism failing him. He gestured toward the ER. "We'll stay with her until she's airlifted."

The doctor glanced at her watch, then turned toward the sounds of the approaching siren. "Here's her ride. We're transporting to the airstrip via ambulance. And because you can't get onto the airfield grounds, the most sensible thing for you guys to do is start driving."

Alyssa's frantic expression propelled Trent to the role of decision maker again. "We'll head out after we kiss her goodbye."

The doctor nodded.

Alyssa edged alongside the bed first. She bent and whispered something in Cory's ear.

No response.

Trent's throat tightened.

"She's sedated."

"Can she hear me?" Alyssa lifted her gaze. The resolute look on her face broke Trent's heart.

"Probably."

Trent wasn't sure if the doctor was being sincere or placating. Either way, Alyssa nodded and stepped back, allowing Jaden room. He leaned into the small bed and tapped his fisted knuckles against his sister's tiny hand, a sportsman's gesture of respect. "Get better. How're you gonna learn to be my wide receiver if you're sick, huh?"

His words undid Alyssa. Trent watched helplessly as quiet tears ran unabashed down her face. Anger at his inability to help choked him.

As they started to head out, the doctor waved a hand toward Trent. "You can say goodbye, too, Dad. You'll see her again in a couple of hours."

Dad.

He met Alyssa's look, expecting chastisement or correction. She inclined her chin toward the bed and paused, waiting.

Trent moved forward, hesitant, his normal confidence shaken by this sudden turn of events. He bent and canvassed Cory's tiny features.

Her color was better, but the tiny girl lying there, intubated and hooked to monitors was a shadow of the funny, winsome child he'd come to know and love.

Love?

Yes. Love. The reality banked Trent's inner fire, the core of a soldier. Despite what might seem impossible or improbable between him and Alyssa, he'd fallen in love with the kid the first time he saw her, when she peered through the upper rails of the playground and called, "Mr. Man?"

The rounded cheeks, the mop of soft gold curls, the big blue eyes, closed now, bright with impish, innocent delight when open. The way it felt when she cradled his cheeks between two tiny hands. He'd missed the years of total wonder and innocence with Jaden. No way did he want to miss it with Cory. He bent closer, swept a kiss to her cheek and whispered, "Hang tight, kid. We got your back."

He cringed, thinking his words were stupid. Worse, knowing they were overheard. He straightened, turned toward Alyssa and Jaden and took a deep breath. "Let's go."

They headed toward the parking lot while the transport team took over. Trent had followed the ambulance in his car. He nodded toward it as the remote locks clicked open. "We can head up in this, then your parents or I can bring your car up to you tomorrow."

"I can drive."

Trent wasn't about to argue or give in. He opened her door, raised his gaze heavenward and waited, not meeting her look. She humphed and slid into the car, obviously displeased by the lack of control.

Because he mirrored that displeasure, he'd keep words to a minimum. He was unaccustomed to feeling helpless, and loss of control was out of sync for a soldier, but they had no choice. So be it.

Jaden hopped into the backseat.

Trent headed up Route 19, then turned up the winding road leading to Alyssa's parents' home. "Why did you turn?" Alyssa pivoted in her seat. "Go back. Head for the Interstate."

"It'll take five minutes for you and Jay to grab what you need from your parents' place," Trent told her. He tapped the steering column. "And this baby rockets, so getting you to Rochester quickly won't be a problem."

"But—"

"No buts." He angled his way into Gary and Susan's driveway.

"Go grab your stuff, tell your dad what's going on and save your mother a lot of wasted time later. She's got to be frantic."

An easier expression softened Alyssa's features as his words registered. She breathed deeply and gave a short nod. "You're right." She wrenched open the door and levered the seat to allow Jaden's exit. "We'll be right back."

"I'll grab gas while you're packing."

"Okay."

Trent backed out of the driveway and headed to the gas station. The five minutes would stretch to ten, he knew that, but he knew Alyssa would feel better in Rochester if she had clean clothes and a toothbrush, the fundamentals that helped ease strife in stressed-out situations. He dialed Helen Walker's number once the tank was filled and explained the situation to her. "I'll be in tomorrow once I'm back here."

"If you need time, Trent, take it."

"Thank you, but that's impossible right now. I've got my laptop in the trunk, so I can make progress, but some things need to be done from the office."

"Then give us what you can in person and do what you can off-site."

Her common sense, family-oriented approach made him breathe a sigh of relief. And it wasn't even his family they were talking about. Not entirely anyway.

But it felt like his family. Jaden, such a good kid, a chip off the old block in so many ways. Cory, her sweet innocence a spark of light that brightened his world of electronic military systems. While his life had been all about battleground strategies and a winning mentality, Cory's had been about teddy bears and bwankies. Her favorite ice creams. *"...and not just banilla either,"* she'd firmly told him.

His throat thickened. His jaw went tight. He fought down emotions that barreled up from twenty-five years of seclusion, when the local police chief had come to his foster home to ask him questions about Clay, and then showed him a picture of Clay's still, lifeless form.

His heart had broken in that fleeting moment of recognition, his brother's features darkened in death, the innocent, gray-eyed little boy with golden brown curls gone forever, a victim of their parents' callous disregard.

He was helpless then.

He was strong now.

And yet...

There was precious little he could do to change the outcome of Cory's illness. That was between the doctors and God. What he could do, he realized as he headed back to pick up Alyssa and Jay, was make Alyssa and their son as comfortable as possible during this time of crisis. He'd witnessed Jay's emotional goodbye and knew firsthand what the boy was going through.

He'd do whatever proved necessary to ease their worry. He might not be part of Alyssa's family per se, but he was a big part of Jay's and that made him one of the main players. Whether Alyssa liked it or not.

Chapter Seventeen

The dark, still house sent a ribbon of alarm snaking down Susan's spine as she pulled into their driveway minutes after Alyssa, Trent and Jaden had left for Rochester.

Steel-toned clouds had encroached, the midday warmth vanquished by a late-season cold front, dark, grim and gray. Heavy rains were expected for the next forty-eight hours, and that always curbed business at the restaurant.

Concerned by the lack of illumination, Susan hurried inside, flicked on the kitchen light and headed for the stairs to check on Gary.

He stood motionless in the living room, facing the picture window overlooking the sloping side yard, his gaze out-turned, his expression blank.

"Gary?"

He frowned and blinked but didn't answer.

Susan laid her hand along his forearm. "You okay?"

The frown deepened, forming a ridge between his eyes. Eyes that looked suspiciously damp. Susan gave his arm a little squeeze. "Come sit down."

He shook her off. "I'm fine."

He wasn't. Not by a long shot. But Susan knew to pick her battles. "You're scared."

"I'm not scared. I'm angry."

"At?"

"God. Me. Everybody."

She touched his arm again. "She'll be fine, Gary."

He scowled and shrugged off her grip again. "You don't know that."

"I believe it."

The scowl deepened.

"I do. With all my heart. She has a problem and they'll fix it. And then she'll be back home with us, right where she belongs."

A tear tracked along Gary's wide, gruff cheek. A single tear, snaking a slow path down beard-roughened skin.

Susan's heart melted but she held tough. Reckoning didn't come without pain, and she and Gary had been around the block, with opposite opinions, over issues with Alyssa for a long time. Maybe…just maybe…

"It's my fault."

"Your fault? How?"

"Cory. This heart thing. I obviously passed my bad ticker on to her and now she's got to suffer for it."

"One might have absolutely nothing to do with the other. You know that, Gary."

"But it could," he insisted. "First I alienate my daughter so that she runs off for a dozen years, then I pass on bad genes to my granddaughter, a tiny, innocent little thing who never…" he choked up, his face crumbling, his jaw slackening, "…ever says a bad thing about anyone. Or anything. Just a little slip of sweetness and light…"

The first tear was joined by several others.

Susan gripped his arm, fear muscling from within. It wouldn't pay to get Gary all upset with his recent heart history, but this internal struggle had been a long time coming. Father and daughter were cut from the same stubborn cloth, and if it took a crisis to knock some sense into both their heads, well…that's how life played out sometimes.

As long as the crisis was solvable, Susan mentally amended.

"Sit down. Please. You having a relapse won't do anyone any good, Gary Langley, and Alyssa needs us to be strong for her."

"She needs you." Gary offered the correction point blank, matter-of-fact. "She hasn't needed me in a long, long time."

"You're wrong." Susan stepped in front of him, blocking the window, forcing him to look at her. "She's always needed you. She just never felt like she measured up. That's partly her fault, and partly yours, but we've got a perfect opportunity now to make things right. She's here and she's ours. Let's not do anything that pushes her away again. This is our chance to show how much we love her, just as she is."

Her words paused him. He stared beyond her shoulder, then dropped his gaze to hers. "I let her think she wasn't good enough."

Susan refused to placate or pretend. "Sometimes. But that's in the past. Let's join forces and deal with the future. Be the parents she needs right now."

Gary swiped a hand across his cheek. "She's been doing a great job up at the restaurant."

Susan nodded. "She has, but that's no surprise, Gary. Running that place is like breathing to Alyssa. It's inborn. And we were foolish not to see that sooner."

He weighed her words, then nodded. "You're right."

Susan fought the urge to tell him she'd been right all along. Not the time or the place. But when all was said and done, with Cory back home and thriving, she'd be glad to remind Gary that stubborn old coots would do well to listen to their wives more often. "Come on. Let's get some sleep. You look exhausted. Alyssa will call if there's any news. They'll evaluate Cory in the morning and we'll know more. And I can drive you up there to see her, okay?"

"Shouldn't we go now?"

A big part of Susan wanted to do just that, but she shook her head, considering Gary's health. "No. Tomorrow. The doctor said she's resting comfortably at the moment. Let's give them time to do their job."

Gary's look of helplessness tugged at her heart, but Susan hardened it. They hadn't gotten to this place without a fair bit of Gary's bullheaded know-it-all nature paving the way. A little penance for past sins wasn't a bad thing. No matter how much his angst clutched at her fix-it-fast mothering side.

She'd hoped for their reconciliation for years. She'd prayed and worried, trying her best to put it in God's hands, knowing shared traits pitted father against daughter. But she knew a lot of that was Gary's fault for trying to make Alyssa something she wasn't. Maybe now they'd have a chance to mend the family ties that had been wrenched apart by plain old obstinacy. She followed Gary upstairs, refusing to sympathize too much. It was long past time for father and daughter to find equal footing. If shared worry over Cory's illness provided that even ground, that wouldn't be a bad thing. As long as Cory came out all right.

"Let's talk out here." The white-coated doctor headed into a hallway brightened by muraled maple trees with three-dimensional animals scattered along the walls. His tight expression validated their concern. Alyssa slipped an arm around Jay's waist, but she'd tapped into some kind of amazing internal maternal reserve on the ride up. She looked better, more stoic than she had in Wellsville.

"First things first. She's got an RSV."

"A what?"

The doctor faced Trent. "A respiratory virus. It's like a cold, but in Cory's case, with her heart problems, this has turned into a significant episode with one thing exacerbating the other. So first we get rid of the virus. It needs to run its course. She's got accompanying pneumonia, so we'll treat her for that as well. This could take several days or longer." He shrugged. "It's hard to tell with kids. The good thing is you caught it early and that gives us an advantage."

"What happens once she gets over this virus?"

"Surgery." He met Alyssa's gaze and tapped the clipboard in his hand. "The tests show that Cory's got a ventricular septal defect, commonly referred to as a VSD. Hers is compounded by an obstruction or tetralogy. That means there's some form of obstruction or narrowing in the pulmonary valve, the one leading from the heart to the lungs. Because of the ventricular defect, Cory's blood doesn't get to the lungs efficiently, meaning it doesn't reoxygenate the way it should. That's what gives her the dusky coloring you noticed earlier."

"How did this happen?" Alyssa faced the doctor, but Trent read guilt and anxiety in her face.

So did the doctor. He shook his head. "It was nothing you did or didn't do, although usually these are diagnosed earlier than this. Occasionally they slip through the cracks until they cause a problem like Cory's has. It's a congenital defect. It may be something that runs in the family, it may be an independent anomaly." He shrugged. "In either case it's fixable. It will require a rather lengthy stay."

He gestured behind them where a pleasant-faced woman stood, her calm stance a blessing. "We've got a Daystar House for parents upstairs. While she's in critical care you're welcome to stay there. That way you can be at her side with no concerns for travel. Once she's on the mend we'll move you to the off-site house, a couple of blocks away. And then home."

Trent extended a hand in gratitude. "Thank you, Doctor."

Alyssa repeated the gesture, her voice catching. "We're so grateful for your help."

The doctor accepted the handshakes, then stepped aside. The maternal-looking woman moved forward as the doctor continued, "Melanie will get you settled upstairs. She'll give you the ins and outs, show you around." He reached out a hand of comfort to Alyssa's arm. "This is scary. We know that. We want you comfortable enough to ask questions. Make yourself at home." He withdrew his pager and frowned. "I've got to go. Mel will give you a notebook. Jot down any questions that might occur. We'll be glad to answer them."

Melanie smiled a welcome as he left, held up one finger and

swept them a warm look. "First rule of thumb in a hospital— when at all possible, take the stairs. Come on. Let's get you guys tucked in for the night."

"I hate leaving you here." Trent meant he hated leaving at all, but it wasn't his place to stay. He knew that. Still…

Alyssa's expression said she wasn't all that keen on his leaving either. She swept the living room a glance. "This is lovely, though. And how wonderful to have a facility for parents right in the hospital."

"Amazing." Trent clasped her shoulders with his hands. "Will you be okay?"

Her nod said yes, but her chin gave a different answer before she firmed it, resolute. "As long as she's fine, I'll be fine."

"Then I'll leave and let you get some sleep. Call me if you hear anything, okay? Or if there's a change?"

"Of course."

He started for the door, but paused when she called his name. He swung back. "Yes?"

"You don't have to do all this, you know." She hesitated, uncertain, then waved a hand around, indicating the parental wing, the hospital, the setting. "I mean, I appreciate it, but it's not really your responsibility. I understand that."

"But Jaden is." Trent fought back hurt at her words. He knew Cory wasn't his responsibility. That had been made clear a number of times. He understood Alyssa was off limits as well. She'd been equally straightforward on that point.

But what affected them, affected Jaden, and Jay *was* his responsibility, his beam of light in a convoluted situation that didn't seem to improve with time. A part of him wanted to make it better. Wanted to embrace the situation and be the backbone.

But he didn't have that right, so he just nodded and pretended she hadn't just stabbed him in the gut. He raised his cell phone in the air. "You'll call?"

She nodded. "Promise."

That's all he could ask. He turned and headed into the cold, dank night, the drop in temperature a reminder that spring came capricious to upstate New York. He drove the car around the block to the hotel he'd booked on the ride up, got the key from the night clerk and headed for his room, hoping to crash.

When sleep refused to come he opened his laptop, grateful for Wi-Fi–friendly rooms and proceeded to crank out numbers for a solid proposal that would mark Helen's firm as a new player on the board of military supply houses. The dance of black figures against a white screen finally nudged him to sleep well after midnight, a sleep dogged by images of small children crying out. Needing him. Calling to him.

He awoke stressed and fatigued, the scant hours of rest interrupted by memories, old and new. Tugging on his jacket, he decided it was time to hunt up a church. The sterile hotel room didn't offer the repose he needed, and Trent was schooled enough to realize that setting marked the path for success. He found a sweet old cathedral down the block, open for daily services. He crept in the back door, took a seat along the far wall and let the combination of old lighting and lemon furniture polish soothe his soul. Calm his spirit. He had no idea when he fell asleep, but the buzz of his cell phone awoke him nearly two hours later.

He sat up, surprised, the hard pew not exactly a bastion of comfort. He struggled for the phone, the combining factors of church and cell phone annoyance making him fumble. By the time he had the phone in hand it had stopped ringing and Trent was awake enough to realize he was alone in the aged church but for one old man on the pew in front of him.

Trent swiped a hand through his hair, stood and stumbled through an apology. "Sorry, I must have been more tired than I thought. I fell asleep."

The old man offered a smile of understanding. "At my age, it happens more often than not, son. At yours? Not so much." He stood and held out his hand. "I'm guessing you've got someone sick around the corner."

Trent nodded. "That obvious, huh?"

"Fairly common. Our proximity brings people in. For that

reason alone, we're glad to be here." He followed Trent toward the back of the church, then veered left to a bank of votive candles, tiny lights flickering in the shadowed alcove. "The name?"

"Cory. A little girl. Just three years old. She's got a heart condition. It's bad."

"Ah." The old man lit a wooden skewer and touched the tip to a taller, broader candle in the back row. "For kids we go big. We want them more noticeable."

Trent frowned, then read the rector's teasing look. He smiled back, strangely comforted. "Thank you."

"You're welcome. And feel free to come again as needed. I keep the side door open all the time."

A rarity in these times of trouble. Trent nodded his appreciation. "Thank you again."

"My pleasure. And I'll put Cory on our prayer list. Between the clutch of old women that come by daily and the much younger Sunday school crew, we'll have her covered twelve ways to Sunday."

The old expression coaxed Trent's smile. "I'd appreciate it."

The elderly gentleman nodded understanding, his look appraising. "We soldiers have to stick together, don't we?"

Trent read the truth in the older man's words as soon as he uttered them. There was something in the old-timer's bearing, his manner, the set of his shoulders that defied the curve of time. "Yes, sir, we do."

Chapter Eighteen

"Alyssa, do you need anything? Anything at all? I can send things up with Trent tonight." Gary's cold precluded him and Susan from visiting until either Cory's surgery was complete or Gary was fully recovered. They couldn't risk reinfecting Cory, so Trent had become the go-between, leaving work at four each day, making the two-hour drive to Rochester and returning to Wellsville by midnight, catching six hours of sleep before he started the cycle all over again.

Jaden had refused to leave the first two days, but when time stretched interminable, Alyssa insisted, knowing he'd be better off in Wellsville, practicing football. Running drills with Chris and the guys. Helping at the restaurant. Keeping busy.

"No, Mom, thanks. Having nothing to do is driving me crazy, but the books helped. And tell Maude I have four quilt squares completed and they're not half bad." Maude McGinnity had sent up a learn-to-quilt book along with precut shapes for a blanket in summer garden pinks and greens. "Tell her Cory will love the colors."

"I will." Susan hesitated, then added, "We love you, honey. We wish we could be there."

"Me, too." The depth of feeling surprised Alyssa. After being away for years, she found the alternative much better. Being reunited with her family. Her friends. Her community.

The constant time alone in the hospital allowed opportunity to dwell on her past and she'd promised herself she wouldn't do that anymore. It was hard when she was on her own most of the time, but Trent and Jay would arrive tonight and stay for the weekend. "I've made some friends here. Other parents."

"I'm glad. Any changes today?"

"Yes. She's doing much better. The infection is waning, she's more alert, and it seems like we're winding down. Once they're sure of that, they'll set up her surgery."

"We've got her on every prayer list in town, and a bunch of out-of-town ones as well."

That uplifted Alyssa. She hadn't seen much result of her own prayers over the years, but was that God's fault or hers? Re-examining the past now that she was back home allowed her a different perspective. She'd made mistakes. She knew that. But she no longer felt like God was out to punish her for them. Cory needed her to be strong. Self-reliant. Valiant. In an odd way it felt good to have developed a backbone along the way. Really good.

"You brought chocolates?" Alyssa eyed the boxes from Megan Russo's old-fashioned candy store when Trent arrived that evening. Her eyes went wide. "Trent, I think I love you."

She was messing around. He knew that. But the look on her face when she said the words was priceless. And somewhat telling.

He let it pass, but added the slip to the list of little things he kept tucked in his heart. The first time she reached for his hand at Cory's bedside. The time she let him hold her as she slept, her head tucked against his chest, her hand curled on his chest. He flashed her a smile as if he took it all in stride. "Everybody loves me, Lyss. I'm just that kind of guy."

She smiled at him, a small smile that started at the corners of her mouth and traveled slowly until it blossomed into the real thing, softening her gaze, brightening her eyes, easing the knot of worry between her brows. "Thank you, Trent. For everything."

He didn't plan to hold her. If he had, he'd have most likely thought twice and held himself back, but he refused to think twice. Or even once. He reached out and drew her into his arms, close to his heart, comforting her in the shelter of his embrace, cloaking her with his strength. A sense of contentment enveloped him as he rested his chin against her soft hair, the smell of hospital antiseptic mixing with sweet vanilla and a hint of cinnamon. Soothing. Nice.

"You smell good." He sighed and allowed himself a few more seconds of what he'd missed for more than a decade, the feel of Alyssa in his arms. Right where she should be. He sighed again. "Really good."

"Twent?"

The sweet sound of Cory's voice jump-started his heart.

"Hey, sugarplum. You're awake." Trent eased away from Alyssa and moved to the side of the crib, feeling huge against the small, high-sided bed, delighted she could talk to him, the ventilator tubing removed. "How're you doing?"

"Can I go home? Pwease?"

Oh, man.

His heart twisted, her imploring look hard to resist.

Alyssa moved to the other side of the bed, her expression tender but firm. "Soon, honey. First the doctors have to fix an itty-bitty problem inside you. Once that's done, you can go home with us."

A woman stepped through the doorway. "Miss Langley?"

Alyssa turned. "Yes?"

"I'm Sandy Smith, the pediatric social worker. Can I talk with you?"

Alyssa's smile faded. She nodded, kissed Cory and brought the rail back up to its previous position. "I'll be right back, sugarplum."

"I'll talk to Twent," Cory promised, although the sleepy expression said she may have awakened too soon. Trent watched Alyssa go, her profile somber, torn between wanting to be with her for whatever the social worker needed to say, and not wanting to leave Cory alone.

"She's awake." Jay entered the room, obviously delighted by Cory's improvement. "Hey, kid."

"Jay, your mom's talking with the social worker. Can you hang with Cory while I join her?"

"Sure. Can I toss her around a little?" He flashed a grin to his little sister and flexed his muscles, Hulk-style. She beamed in return, then yawned.

Trent smiled and grabbed Jaden in a half hug. "Let's wait till we get her fixed up, okay? Then we'll wrestle her around again."

"All right." Jaden drew out his tone, feigning reluctance, making Cory laugh. He withdrew an old-style game system from his pocket and handed it over. "You wanna play? There are princesses on all the levels."

Her eyes widened, telling Trent this was momentous, indeed. "Sure. Fank you."

"You're welcome." Jaden grinned down at her. "Go ahead, Dad. We'll be fine here."

Trent halted his steps.

Jay had never called him dad before. He'd been Trent, understandably, and he'd be the last person on earth to push the boy to new levels of their relationship, but the sound of that word coming willingly from Jaden's mouth made the whole day seem brighter. He flashed Jay a smile that said he recognized the change and tipped his gaze down to Cory. "No wrestling. Got it?"

She giggled. "Got it, Twent."

That smile. That face. That total innocence. She had to be all right. She just had to. He wouldn't let what happened to Clay happen to Cory. She was a darling child, a gift from God, a child of light. He'd do whatever proved necessary to make sure she emerged unscathed from this whole business, hale and hearty, ready to embrace the life God meant for her.

And when he stepped through the social worker's door a

moment later, the stack of financial aid forms offered him instant opportunity to make good on his pledge. "She doesn't need to do any of that, ma'am." Respectful, Trent put his hands on Alyssa's shoulders and took his place behind her. He'd missed this with Jay, but the boy was strong beyond the norm. Cory wasn't. He gave Alyssa's shoulders a light squeeze and swept the forms a glance. "I'll guarantee the bill."

"Trent, no—"

"Yes." He squeezed again, then squatted alongside her. "There's no use arguing this, Lyssa. Don't even try. Consider it eleven years of child support I didn't have to pay."

"But…"

"No buts." He turned his gaze toward Sandy. "Do we have a ballpark figure?"

She shook her head. "Not yet, and I was just explaining to Alyssa that she qualifies for certain state programs that will reduce the bill substantially."

"Wonderful. But whatever isn't covered, I'll guarantee. Where do I sign?"

"Trent—"

"Simple retribution, Lyssa. Fair is fair. You gave me a son. Now I get to give you a daughter. The only thing that matters is for Cory to get the treatment she needs, right?"

She didn't hesitate. "Yes."

"Well, then." He leaned over and signed the forms as the social worker indicated, his quick, decisive script making short work of the decision.

The money was inconsequential. He could mortgage the house to cover what he'd pay the hospital, if necessary. He had time. Cory didn't. She needed help now, and the last thing Alyssa needed was to worry herself sick about being in debt for years to come on top of her little girl's compromised heart.

Lack of sleep, Trent's kindness and a dose of female hormones put Alyssa over the top once they'd left Sandy's office. She paused, hugging herself, pretending to look at a bright-toned painting, trying valiantly not to shake.

"Hey."

She shook her head, a plea for time, unable to pull her emotions in line quick enough to waltz into Cory's room like everything was all right.

Strong arms wrapped around her, drawing her close, the beating heart beneath her ear blessedly familiar. She had no idea why he was being so nice to her after what she did with Jay. Why he'd care enough to step in and help with Cory. But having him cocoon her in his grasp, shelter her in his arms had to be the most wonderful feeling she'd ever experienced. And when she tried to pull free, he hung tight, his chin lowered to her hair, his grip snug, the scent of him reminding her of times long past.

"It's okay to cry."

A nurse passed by and handed her a clutch of tissues. Alyssa gave her a weepy half smile and dabbed her eyes. Blew her nose. "I know. I'm just tired. Scared. Nervous. Hormonal."

"Hungry?"

"No."

"I'll tell you what." He loosened his grip and leaned back, meeting her gaze. "There's a family diner across the street. I'll grab some dinner for us, okay? Bring it back here. Jay won't eat if you don't."

She didn't want anything at the moment, but he'd made a good point about Jaden and bringing food in was a good idea. "Okay."

Trent eased back, releasing her. Part of her longed to step back into the curve of his arm, the shelter it afforded. Another part urged her to duck and run. He pressed a platonic kiss to her forehead. Gentle. Reassuring. "God's got your back, Lyss. Twenty-four/seven."

He shouldn't, though. Not after her carelessness with her children.

How many times had she brushed off Cory's ailments as normal childhood afflictions, refusing to take her to the doctor because money was nonexistent? Too many to count. And now...

Trent tipped her chin up. "There's a chapel downstairs and a sweet old church around the corner with a very cool pastor who served in the military. And Army guys never lie. You know that. Ask and you shall receive, Lyssa."

"Words, Trent. Simple words in a nice, old book."

He didn't argue with her. He slipped an arm around her and dropped his forehead to hers, drawing her close once more, his breath tickling her ear as he quoted softly. "We walk by faith, not by sight. One way or another we're going to fill that heart of yours with faith, hope and love."

It sounded good. So good.

But first she'd have to drain the weight of guilt to make room. She'd tried that in the past but to no avail. Did God really hear prayers? Or answer them?

Something in Trent's self-assurance, his strength, his fortitude tempted her to try again. Maybe.

He stepped back, ending the moment. "I'll be back in a few minutes, okay?"

"Okay."

He gave a quick nod and paused by Cory's door on his way out. "Jay, I'm heading across the street to grab food. I'll be right back."

Jaden moved alongside the crib. "Cool. We're just about to watch that Snow Queen movie I love so much."

"Well, who doesn't?" Trent exchanged a manly look of understanding with Jaden, his expression saying he knew the kid was going the distance. Snow Queens. Sheesh.

Trent leaned in and kissed Cory. "You might want a nap, sugarplum."

"I'm not tired, Twent. I just want to go home wif my mommy."

"Soon. I promise. First we have to get you better, okay?" Trent raised a brow to her. "The more you rest, the sooner that will happen. Got it?"

She flashed him a smile of understanding. "Got it. Can I have a milkshake?"

Trent turned a questioning look to Alyssa.

She nodded.

"Chocolate or vanilla?"

"Banilla. Wif cookies."

"Say what?" Trent gave her a mock scowl, noogied her head and headed out. "You're such a girl, Cory. Nothing's simple. Gotta make everything complicated."

The teasing look he sent Alyssa warmed her, inspiring memories of the fun they used to have, the teasing, the joking, the time spent talking about nothing and everything.

She watched him stride away, his upward stance a message of strength and substance, a profile she wanted to emulate.

So... Do it, her inner voice scolded. *Put those shoulders back and stop being a ninny. Set your goals and strive for them. Isn't that what you've taught Jaden to do by word? Now reinforce the lesson by deed. Go for it. What have you got to lose?*

Nothing, she realized. And she didn't want to be a whiner. Or a clinger. Not ever again.

Chapter Nineteen

"Whoa. Cool dog." Jaden grinned as a woman with a large, fluffy dog stopped by Cory's room the next morning. Hands pressed to her mouth, Cory giggled with amazement.

The woman eyed Cory, her manner expectant. "We're feeling better."

Alyssa moved forward while Cory clapped her hands, gleeful. "Can I see him, Mommy? Pwease? He's so beee-u-tiful. And big and hairy," she added. She stood in the crib, arms out, imploring.

The woman stretched a hand to Alyssa. "I'm Lynn DiMaggio. And this—" she dropped her gaze to the well-behaved ragamuffin pooch at her side "—is Bear."

Alyssa reached out a hand to the dog. "Appropriate. He resembles a bear."

"That's a funny name, Mommy," Cory chortled from her spot across the room. "Can I pet him?"

"May I pet him," Alyssa corrected.

Cory huffed a sigh, making her look all that much healthier, the hint of attitude an odd comfort. "May I pet him?"

Lynn smiled. "You may if you're cleared to come to the playroom. Is she?" Lynn queried a nurse from the nearby station who nodded.

The nurse came in and helped Jaden settle Cory into a

wheelchair. Alyssa tucked Cory's favorite blanket around her legs, then followed the woman and dog to the brightly lit playroom down the hall.

"Mommy, look! A monkey!"

Alyssa grinned. The children's play stations and throw rugs reflected jungle-muraled walls. The room engaged the senses, a kids' room. From the looks of the three children already gathered there, Bear was no stranger. Given his shaggy coat and size, he melded with the surrounding theme.

Alyssa sat on the floor alongside Cory's chair and invited Bear over. He came carefully, as if understanding the frailties of the children in this room. When Lynn raised a cupped hand, Bear sat, politely waiting to be petted, his bright eyes and happy grin the perfect icebreaker. Cory leaned forward, sinking small fingers into soft, silky curls. "Can we get a dog, Mommy? Pwease?"

"We don't have room for a dog, sugarplum."

"He could sweep wif me," Cory explained, earnest. "My bed is big enough for me and a dog."

"Dogs are a big responsibility." Lynn settled into the chair alongside Cory. She sent Alyssa a smile of understanding. The other kids circled around, including a little boy whose bald head offered mute testimony to chemotherapy, while his bright smile reflected a youngster's natural curiosity. "Bear needs to be brushed, walked, fed and taken to the vet now and again. And I have to clean up his poops outside."

"Eeeewwwwwww…" A little girl plugged her nose. "We have a dog, but my daddy does that job."

Cory leaned closer. "If I had a daddy, could I get a dog? Pwease?"

Lynn's quick look of empathy apologized for putting Alyssa in an awkward spot. A voice from the door interrupted the conversation. "How about if you had a nice Grandpa? I like dogs, peanut."

Cory turned, excited. "Gwandpa! And Gwammy! My fever is gone and I'm almost all better!"

"An answer to my prayers." Susan bent and kissed Cory's cheek. "You like this big, ol' dog, peanut?"

"I wuv him." Cory lifted an imploring gaze to Susan that shifted then to Gary. "Could we get a dog, Gwandpa, you and me? Then we could share him."

"Think before you speak, Gary." Susan settled a wifely look of caution on Alyssa's father. "This could come back to haunt you."

He arched a mock gruff brow in her direction, then slid a wink to Cory. "It makes perfect sense, Grammy, don't you think?" He slanted a teasing look to his wife as he crouched alongside the bald-headed boy. "Before Alyssa came back with the kids, I was knee-deep in work night and day. A man my age likes to take a breather now and again."

Alyssa pretended to be cleaning her ears. "Excuse me? Who are you and what have you done with my father?"

Gary gave her a comfortable nod as if handing over the reins was a natural, normal circumstance in the Langley house.

Hah.

But her father bore an ease of manner she'd forgotten existed. A comfort she hadn't seen since childhood.

"Now that we have another manager on hand, it makes sense for me to spend more time at home with Cory. And a dog. Did you know dogs love to fish?" he asked Cory, matter-of-fact.

"Really?"

"Oh, yes." Gary nodded, his eyes teasing, but a shadow of worry softening his jaw as he gave Cory a thorough once-over. "And a lot of dogs love to swim."

"Me, too," Cory attested, serious.

"Well, that's perfect," proclaimed Gary. "Once you're home again, you and I will go dog shopping."

"For a puppy?"

Gary shook his head. "No puppies. I think a dog that's a little older but young enough to still train up. Puppies are cute but they jump and scratch. They're hard for little girls to handle." He sent a look to Bear's owner. "How old is Bear?"

"Nearly four," she told him.

"And he's a…?"

"Golden Doodle," she replied.

"But…"

Lynn smiled and inclined her head. "Golden just means he's a cross with a Golden Retriever. Doodles can be lots of colors. Bear happens to be black."

"I really like black dogs," the young boy told them with an erstwhile expression. "I think black dogs are my favorite."

"I like them, too." Gary gave Bear one last pat before he stood, his wince lamenting aging knees.

Cory yawned, not once, but twice.

"All right, sugarplum, say goodbye to everyone. Time for you to have a little rest."

"I'm not tired."

"Oh, I know." Alyssa smiled and wheeled Cory to the sink so they could wash up.

Gary leaned down, reached into his pocket and withdrew a blue-and-white box. "I brought cards along. How 'bout you and I have a game of war?"

"And we can play Memory!" Cory's voice hiked up before she stifled another yawn, her tiredness a reminder that all was not well.

But it would be, Alyssa told herself. Seeing her father's more relaxed attitude, his softer demeanor an unusual gift, she could almost make herself believe it.

Trent stopped in Helen's office before heading to Rochester on Monday. "I've got the preliminary work complete for the new bid we're proposing to NAWC. We should be able to submit the formal version once we're in final format." He paused briefly. "I'm having Casey fax it to me at the hotel so I can double check everything before we send it on."

"I'm impressed." Helen was the kind of boss you liked to impress, her approval never casually given. "Jeff will stay on top of things here. Call and let us know how tomorrow's surgery goes, all right?"

"Will do."

She waved her preliminary copy of the bid. "I'll go over this tonight and call you tomorrow if I have questions. If your cell phone is off, I'll e-mail you. We're good."

"Thanks, Helen." He turned and headed for the door, knowing the two-hour ride would give him plenty of time to take care of phone calls he'd put off to complete his hands-on work on the bid.

Once he'd handled his business calls with an officer's bent for professionalism, he hit a button to call Alyssa. She answered on the first ring, her tone slightly out of breath as though hurrying. Was there a problem? Or was she just glad he called?

"Fill me in."

Oops. Business mode. He changed tactics in quick style. "Wait, back up. Let's start again, okay? Hey, Lyss, how's everything going? How's Cory? Fill me in."

"We're on the schedule for seven-thirty tomorrow. We can stay with her until she falls asleep, and then…" Her voice caught for just a moment, as though tripping on emotion. "And then we wait. And pray."

Open-heart surgery… On such a little bit of a thing. Trent swallowed hard, trying to separate Clay and Cory, two beautiful three-year-olds, both of whom deserved a chance at a full, happy life.

Clay's chance had been denied him.

Cory's wouldn't be.

"Do you or Jay need anything, Lyss? I can swing by the mall off Route 390."

"We're good, thanks. Mom and Dad did a shopping run earlier. They've set up camp at your hotel. I hope that's okay." Her slight hesitation told him she was concerned about her father and him sharing the same two-hundred-room hotel.

He wasn't worried. Gary would have to deal with him regularly now that they all shared a town and a relationship through

Jaden. Maybe Cory's crisis would provide a natural bridge for that to happen. Then he remembered the look Gary shot him when he brought Jaden home the week before, and realized that might not be the case.

Regardless, they were brought together in a common cause: Cory's well-being. If nothing else, that should unite them at least temporarily.

"I'll be there in a little bit," he told Alyssa as he passed a sign for Geneseo. "Call if you need anything."

"I will."

She hung up her cell phone and stared out the window, considering his words, wishing she could tell Trent just what she needed—him. And a second chance at the future she'd thrown away a dozen years ago. What would her life have been if she hadn't hidden Jaden? Would they have ended up like so many young couples, burned out and divorced a few years later? She shrugged into a sweater and checked to see if Cory was still asleep.

She was. Gary slept alongside her in the foldout chair, while Jaden and the bald boy from around the corner of the nurses' station played a two-man computer game system. Alyssa interrupted her mother's reading. "I'm going to take a little walk."

Susan nodded. "The chapel's downstairs."

"You sound like Trent."

"Smart guy," her mom murmured.

"Yeah. Well." Alyssa lifted a shoulder in a half shrug. "I just need some air."

"Of course, honey. I'll be right here."

She'd texted Aunt Gee about Cory's hospitalization. Once outside, she saw the waiting voice mail on her cell phone and called Gee back. "Hey."

Gee's voice brought back a boatload of memories, some good, some bad. "Hey, kiddo, how's our little girl doing?"

"Better. They're operating tomorrow. The doctor is wonderful and he says it's quite fixable, but…"

"But?"

"It's still heart surgery. And she's still my baby."

"I know. Alyssa, I'm so sorry. How's Jaden?"

Alyssa drew a deep breath. "Amazingly strong. He seems to thrive off Trent's strength and then feeds it back. He's convinced she'll be fine." A note of irony filled her voice. "And he's not as mad at me about taking him away from his father now that he's got Cory to worry about. Kind of put things in perspective, I guess."

"Or just nudged it into the background." Gee paused a moment. "And Trent? How is he?"

"About the most amazing and wonderful man in the entire world," Alyssa confessed.

"Oh dear."

"Exactly."

"So, what do you do now?" Gee asked.

"Nothing." Alyssa firmed her voice and her shoulders. "I work and take care of my kids the way I should have all along."

"Alyssa, you always took care of those children," Gee argued. "When money was tight, you went without. When the chips were down, you stayed upbeat. You tried your best."

"I partied when Jaden was a baby and stayed with Vaughn way too long," Alyssa countered. "If I hadn't tried so hard to believe him—"

"None of us wants to doubt the people we care about." Gee's voice softened. "You need to step outside the situation and see it for what it really was. Vaughn was good at working a room, instilling belief. He had a lot of us fooled. How is any of that your fault?"

"I could have told someone. You. The pastor in town. The police."

"Why didn't you?"

The question of the hour, a dynamic so foolishly skewed it might point to mental instability. Alyssa couldn't face that now. Wouldn't face that now. Why was she so needy that she desperately wanted to believe Vaughn's promises?

"I have to go, Gee."

"God bless you, honey. I'm praying for you and Cory. For her quick healing."

Not too long ago Alyssa would have brushed off prayers for herself, but as Gee uttered the words, Alyssa recognized another change. It felt good to have people care about her. Concerned about her. She saw it in her mother's eyes. In her father's more gentle bearing. In Pastor Hannity's gaze when he drove up to visit her and offer solace. "Thanks, Gee. We'll talk again soon."

She hung up the phone, turned back toward the hospital entrance and ran into Trent.

"Lyssa?" He grabbed her upper arms to steady her. "I didn't expect to see you out here."

"Hey. Sorry." She stepped back, brushed loose tendrils of hair from her face and grimaced a look to the hospital. "Cory's sleeping, Mom's with her and I needed some air."

His smile said he understood. "Plenty of that out here. Want to walk a little?"

Oh, she did. Gazing up into those gorgeous eyes, she wanted desperately to accept his invitation. But she was close to growing dependent again. She felt the urge and fought to keep it at bay. She'd promised herself to never be dependent on a man again. To never be under someone's thumb. She'd come back to Jamison determined to work herself into a position of independence. It's what she wanted. What she needed.

But when he tilted his head, a little smile coaxing his lips, warming his eyes, she gave a quick nod. "I'd like that."

Her inner voice scolded a warning.

Alyssa shut it down.

Walking with Trent was a little thing. Nothing to get all hung up about. And yet…

When he reached down and clasped her fingers, his thumb making gentle circles along the back of her hand, she realized that strolling with Trent *was* something to get all hung up about. Something she'd like to do on a regular basis, say, like… forever?

He squeezed her hand lightly. "This brings back memories."

"It does. Trent…"

"Save it, Lyss. I'm just enjoying a few minutes of quiet time with a pretty girl. No law against that."

"Maybe there should be."

He laughed and shoulder nudged her. "Scared?"

"Yes."

Her honesty surprised him. He stopped walking and turned to face her, lifting her chin with his free hand so their eyes met, doubt searing his voice. "Of me?"

"No." She drew a breath, then raised their joined hands. "Of this. Of taking chances. Of messing with Jaden's head and heart."

She didn't say "again," but Trent heard the inference as if she'd uttered it out loud. He nodded, brought her hand up to his mouth and pressed a gentle kiss to the thin, soft skin along the back, days of dishwashing and table scrubbing taking their toll. "You're right."

She looked relieved at his words, but he refused to leave it at that. "To a degree, which only means we take things slowly. One step at a time."

"Or not at all."

He studied her, sensing her reluctance…seeing her longing, wanting to comfort both. "I don't think that's an option any more, Lyss."

"It's the only option, Trent."

"Well, there's this—" Slipping their joined hands around her waist, he drew her in, not leaving her time to reconsider. He let his lips brush hers gently at first, tender and imploring. It was a kiss of old times and first loves, of times remembered and times to come, a kiss that deepened of its own accord as she stepped into his embrace.

In those precious seconds, Trent's world righted itself. He'd worked hard to get where he was, an industrious goal setter whose expertise could help so many others, but as noble as that seemed, it paled in comparison to finding Alyssa again.

"We can't do this."

"Just did." He rubbed small circles on her back, holding her close to his heart, his chin on her hair again, recognizing perfection. "And it was quite nice."

"Trent."

"I know." He edged back and met her gaze, wanting to ease the troubled look that darkened her gaze. "We have other things to concern ourselves with right now. Cory and Jaden. But this—" he waved a hand between them "—isn't about to go away. We can shelve it for a while, but it won't disappear. You know that, right?"

She knew a lot of things. Too much. Gazing up at the strong, upright man facing her, a part of her longed to step into that embrace again, to lose herself in the feel of someone caring for her. For all of them.

But she'd made too many mistakes to take this at face value. Thoughts of Vaughn's loving words and gentle touch, his easy cowboy charm, tipped the scales in Trent's disfavor.

She knew Trent wasn't Vaughn. What she didn't know is why her internal neediness proved her undoing time and again. Until she figured that out, she couldn't risk involvement. She'd promised herself independence and strength. She'd be wrong to let anything interfere with that goal.

"I'm not looking for this, Trent. I've got way too much baggage to be good for anyone right now. I'm vulnerable because of Cory's illness. I get that." She stepped back. "But I've got to prioritize and right now my priority is Jaden's well-being and Cory's health, both of which I've managed to mess up royally."

He put his hands up. "Understood. We'll take this up at a later date."

"Or be smart and realize we had our chance and I blew it."

"We blew it," he reminded her, walking close to her side but not touching her. "You had help. Do you ever wonder what would have happened if I knew, Lyss? What our life would have been like?"

Countless times, but she wasn't going to admit that. "It is what it is, Trent. No sense chasing shadows."

"So we move forward." He caught her hand outside the hospital door and held her there for just a moment. "We let God and time guide our paths."

She'd disappointed herself and God too often to find that choice appealing, but something in Trent's warmth and assurance carved a niche in her toughened hide. "You think he cares?"

"I know he does." Trent squeezed her hands, his expression knowing. Almost peaceful. "You think our paths ended up back here at the same time by accident? By coincidence?" He shook his head, confident. "It might have been a broken road, but that was our fault. Not his." He dropped her hands, smiled and reached around her to open the heavy entrance door. "Prayer and time. We've got both."

He made it sound easy. Like they could go back to where they'd left off a dozen years past, start anew with a clean slate.

She knew better. She understood retribution. Reprisal. While Trent had served his country honorably, creating a stellar academic and military record, she'd patchwork-pieced her life, forgetting the basic rule of building was a strong foundation.

She'd continue to build that foundation now, once Cory recovered. She was in her element working at The Edge. She just needed her father to see that, to understand what they'd both tried to deny all those years ago: She didn't thrive on academia. She'd never wanted to be a cheerleader or valedictorian. She'd barely made honor roll and that was only with diligent work and Trent's encouragement and study help.

But she loved the restaurant business. She relished the hustle and bustle of a dinner rush, of jumping roles at a moment's notice, donning an apron, preparing specials, working the front door on a crazy-busy Friday night. Then when the work was all done and she finally shut the lights down at the end of a long day, she felt deeply satisfied by how she and the staff had responded to every need.

Reverend Hannity had homilized about gifts and talents last week, about how St. Paul viewed the church as the people within, living and breathing with individual gifts of the Spirit, their talents unique and special.

When she ran shift at The Edge, she felt special. She felt… empowered. On top of things. Was that weird?

She didn't know. But she knew it felt good, as if she belonged there, making snap decisions, welcoming new customers and old, ensuring that their evening was special.

Maybe that wasn't what the good reverend meant at all, but it made sense to Alyssa. Glancing up at Trent she smiled, his consideration a blessing.

His return expression said he read her thoughts, the little smile a mix of teasing and smugness, as if he read the future and she was in it.

But that was only because he didn't know her past.

Dropping her gaze, she moved forward, eyes straight ahead, remembering Gee's words of absolution. Maybe it wasn't her fault that Liliana's ashes lay in a tiny, sealed box tucked in her dresser. But it sure felt like her fault.

Chapter Twenty

Noting the scrub-draped doctor's rapid approach at noon on Tuesday, Trent reached for Alyssa's hand and squeezed.

Chin up, eyes trained ahead, she didn't look his way.

But she squeezed back, her gesture saying she recognized they were in this together.

"Everything went quite well." The surgeon faced Alyssa, but slid a smile toward Jaden as if recognizing the youngster's fears. "We were able to make the repair. The heart muscle is undamaged, and the valve obstruction was minimal which means she shouldn't need further surgeries." He turned to face Alyssa. "We'll schedule follow-up appointments to make sure things are fine as she matures, but I'm optimistic."

"And being discovered this late?" Alyssa hesitated, as if choosing her words with care. "Did that put her in extra danger?"

The doctor shrugged. "Who's to say? Sometimes these things go unnoticed for a while. The important thing is we found it, fixed it, and she's going to be fine."

Trent keyed into Alyssa's question, wondering.

She felt guilty about Cory's problem. Why? Reverend Hannity's counsel about how women mantle guilt around their shoulders came back to him once more. He released her hand and slipped an arm around her shoulders, bracing her. "When can we see her?"

"Later." The surgeon swiped an arm across his brow, frowned at the clock and shrugged. "She'll be in recovery for a while. Go grab some lunch. Take a walk. The nurses tell me it's beautiful outside. The girls at the desk have your number, right?" He waved toward the surgical hospitality desk.

"Yes."

"If you're not back, we'll call as soon as she can entertain visitors."

"Doctor—" Alyssa paused, her voice tight "—thank you."

He smiled and shook her free hand. "You're welcome."

Gary slung an arm around Jaden's shoulders. "Lunch is on me. Let's go celebrate."

Alyssa glanced at the surgical unit doors, reluctant.

Susan intercepted the look. "Stop borrowing trouble. You heard what the doctor said. We should be rejoicing, not worrying."

Alyssa met her mother's look, made a face, then smiled. "You're right, of course. This is exactly what we prayed for. I just can't wait to see her."

"Does this mean we're going to spoil her even more than we do already?" Jaden posed the question to the entire group as they approached the elevator. "Because I'd be okay if we didn't."

Trent jabbed his shoulder, teasing. "You jealous of a little girl?"

Jaden met his grin, his eyes more relaxed than they'd been in days. "I'm just glad she's going to be all right."

The sincerity in his voice made Susan nod, Gary sniffle and Alyssa tear up. She leaned into Jaden's side and gave him a quick hug. "Me, too."

"Everything's ready?" Trent met Gary's eyes as he scanned the porch, tamping nerves with little luck.

Gary sent Trent a knowing look. "Worried?"

"No. Yes. No."

Gary smiled and nodded toward Jay as he dashed out of the house. "He'll keep your mind off things."

Trent couldn't disagree. They'd decided to have Susan and

Alyssa bring Cory home while Trent and Gary kept Jaden occupied, but at this moment Trent regretted the decision. He wanted to be there to scoop Cory up, tuck her in her car seat, listen to her tiny voice butchering selected consonants as they navigated the roads to Jamison. He longed to share this moment of triumph with Alyssa, but he was beginning to understand that once you had more than one kid, priorities were often split.

He grabbed a football, shouted, "Go deep!", then lofted the ball to Jaden's left. The boy scrambled, raced, darted an over-the-shoulder look that rivaled the best of the best and did a Lynn Swan–like stretch to pull the ball into his chest at the last possible moment.

Trent grinned. "Not bad."

Jaden burst out laughing, a sound Trent welcomed. Jay didn't laugh as much as the other guys his age. Nature? Nurture?

Trent wasn't sure, but hearing his laughter today, knowing how much better Jay felt because Cory was on the mend, sweetened the deal.

Gary stood. "You guys want something to drink?"

Jaden gave his grandfather a rock-on fist pump. "Gatorade would be great."

Gary inclined his head Trent's way. "Same for you?"

"Please."

"Done." Turning briskly, Gary headed inside.

Trent watched him go, noting his stride looked stronger. More assured. He appeared thinner, too, a trait that would please his cardiologist. But more than the physiological, Trent recognized a distinct change in Gary's attitude. He seemed less confrontational. Less antagonistic. Knowing that Alyssa and Gary would be home together caring for Cory while Susan and Jaden took over at The Edge, Trent was glad to see the shift in temperament. Lyssa had inevitably locked horns with her father as a kid, often with good reason, but it would be nicer for everyone if they maintained a truce for a while. A long while.

A short time later Susan's SUV pulled into the driveway, pausing near the front door.

Balloons decorated the small front porch, beneath a banner that read "Welcome Home, Cory!" in bright pink font. They'd decided to keep Cory in the main house until she'd recovered sufficiently to do the garage stairs on a regular basis, so Jaden and Trent had moved her bed into the well-lit living room where a crew of stuffed animals, toys and dolls waited their owner's return.

"Twent! I'm home!"

"You sure are, sugarplum." Trent bit back a ball of emotion as he undid her seat belt harness and lifted her from the car. Did she feel lighter? More frail?

She planted two tiny hands alongside his cheeks, squeezed and then leaned in and kissed his mouth. "I missed you so much! And Gwandpa, too! And Jay, too!"

Frail? Not a bit.

Trent hugged her close, laughing his relief. "Well, it's good to know we were missed, sugarplum, and as soon as you're better, there's work to be done."

"Oh, I know." She nodded sage agreement as he headed toward the porch. "I haven't done my numbers or my puzzles in a long, long time and I fink my bwain wants to do some."

"Soon," Alyssa promised. She met Trent's smile with a grin that further lightened his heart. She nodded toward Cory. "This is what we've dealt with for two solid hours of driving."

Susan made a yap-yap-yap sign with her left hand. "I think her shut-off valve is broken. She hasn't stopped the entire way. Or even considered slowing down."

Cory peeked at Susan over Trent's shoulder. "Gwammy, I have so much to say! I've been missing being home this much!" She threw her arms wide, narrowly missing Trent's face and squarely socking her grandfather in the side of the head. "Oops. Sorry, Gwandpa!"

He took her from Trent's arms, his gaze suspiciously moist. "It's all right. I'm tough. What do you think about this porch, huh?"

"I fink it is the most beeee-u-tiful porch in the whole wide world," she told him, earnest. "I wuv the balloons and the wib-bons, and the words, but most of all, I wuv you, Gwandpa." She tucked her arms around Gary's broad neck and squeezed. "I missed you so much."

Gary worked to firm his chin and his voice at her innocent pronouncement, then sent a gruff look toward the gathered adults, all watching with more than a hint of amazement. "Something in my eye," he muttered, brushing a free hand across his face.

Susan rolled her eyes and stepped through the front door. "Of course, dear. Hey, Miss Cory, come in here. See what's waiting for you."

Cory's eyes went round and wide as she surveyed the trans-formed living room. "My friends are here!"

"They've been waiting for you." Alyssa touched her forehead to Cory's and stepped back. "Missing you."

"And I've been missing them," Cory agreed, nodding. She wriggled to get down. Gary sent a look of question Alyssa's way.

"The doctor said she can do whatever she wants within reason. He said her body will be her best guide, that children are smart enough to lie down and take a nap when needed, unlike adults."

Susan harrumphed.

Gary ignored her.

"Diet restrictions?" Trent posed the question to Alyssa as Cory sank to the thick carpet, drawing a group of lonely stuffed animals into a close circle.

"None. She'll be on meds for a little while, and will need to have antibiotics when she has dental procedures, but at her age that might be a nonissue. And she has her follow-up appointment with the nurse practitioner next week and then the cardiologist in late July." Alyssa smiled. "She's bouncing back quickly, accord-ing to the entire staff of the hospital."

"Bouncing being the operative word of the day." Susan grinned at Jaden, whose relieved expression revealed just how worried he'd been. But with Cory obviously better, Jaden's countenance relaxed. And while Trent knew Jaden shouldn't feel responsible for his sister's welfare, he also recognized the loving soul within his son. But undeserved guilt often accompanied a conscientious spirit, and Trent knew the plusses and minuses of that firsthand.

"Jay, can you grab the overnight bags from the trunk?"

"I'll help." Trent followed Jay outside and helped unload the bags.

Jay eyed the bags and frowned, jerking his head toward the garage apartment at the back of the drive. "Our place or Grandma's?"

Trent eyed the bags. "Here? To do laundry maybe?"

"Makes sense. And if we're wrong, they'll let us know right off. They always do."

Trent laughed. "You've got that right." As they headed around back to the laundry room entrance, Trent noted, "Cory sounds good, doesn't she?"

"Real good." Jay's tone revealed his relief. "I prayed a lot while she was sick."

Trent nodded, cautious. Most preteens weren't big on getting prayer lectures, especially from fathers who just showed up on the scene.

"It worked this time."

Meaning it hadn't other times. But when? And for what?

"Garth Brooks sang a song about unanswered prayers," Trent told Jay as he shouldered open the inner door. "About how they can sometimes turn into the best things that happen to us. We just don't always see it at the time."

Jay frowned as if trying to equate Trent's wisdom with his situation and coming up short. Then he shrugged. "I'm just glad she's okay. She's a cool kid. Even if we do spoil her."

"We'll try to minimize that now that she's better."

Alyssa approached them, overhearing, marveling at the resemblance as father and son set down the bags, things that went well beyond appearance. They quirked their jaws and angled their heads the same way, and walked with that same upright stance, an inborn quality of strength.

Trent sent her an easy look. "Not spoiling her would be easier if she wasn't so cute."

"Cute becomes pesky really quick in three-year-olds," Alyssa informed him. "Thanks for bringing these in, guys. Mom and I will sort the wash later, but I wanted to get a quick load of blue jeans going now."

"You're not thinking of working tonight, are you?" Trent stepped forward as Jay headed down the hall toward the kitchen.

"No, but everything I own is dirty. Mom and Jay are going to handle the restaurant this week. Then we'll trade off and on for the next couple of weeks. If I stay home with Cory the entire first half of the summer, we'll drive each other crazy."

"I'd be glad to take a shift," Trent offered.

He'd moved closer, close enough for her to reach up and trace the tiny lines that edged his eyes, eyes that said so much. Maybe too much.

Then again, maybe not.

"I think you're busy enough with work, settling into your house and working with Jay on his football skills."

"I can make time."

He angled his head slightly, eyeing her, his gaze traveling from her eyes to her mouth. Settling there. One second. Now two. Three, four...

He leaned in, brushing a gentle kiss across her mouth that traveled to her cheek, her hair, her temple, then found its way back to where it belonged for long seconds that seemed way too short.

"I—Oh. Um... sorry." Susan's interruption made Alyssa step back, but Trent didn't let go. She sent him a look of chagrin.

"Nothing to apologize for." He kept his grasp on Alyssa's waist light but firm while he sent Susan a smile. "I can't say I'm a bit sorry."

Susan grinned.

A part of Alyssa wanted to deny what her mother witnessed. A very big part, actually.

But another side of her longed to embrace the chance to put things right at long last. To move forward.

Was this what Reverend Hannity meant when he talked about being washed clean? When he referred to stumbling out of the darkness, into the light?

She felt light in Trent's arms. She felt invigorated that she'd prayed for Cory's health and Cory's recovery seemed imminent. She'd prayed for her father's health and his renewed vigor and decrease in acrimony seemed like frosting on the cake.

Why shouldn't she step into this promise of new life, a chance to rekindle her relationship with Trent? He was obviously willing and Trent was a savvy guy with a forgiving nature. He couldn't look at Jay and Cory and think she came without some baggage, right?

He winked, chucked her on the chin, planted a kiss to her forehead and released her with a nod to the suitcases. "All yours, ladies. The kid and I did the muscle stuff. You get the sorting end of the deal."

"Will do." Susan's wholesale smile flashed like a banner of approval.

Alyssa jabbed her in the side as Trent headed for the front room, whistling. "No lectures, okay?"

"Not a one." Susan bent and unzipped the first bag, then began tossing clothes into various baskets, humming the same song Trent had just been whistling, the one he'd referenced about thanking God for unanswered prayers.

Thinking of Cory's road to recovery after a bad scare, Alyssa added thanks for the answered prayers as well. And she decided to stop pretending that Trent wasn't a big part of those answered prayers.

Chapter Twenty-one

Alyssa paused, silent, watching the scene before her, beautiful in its simplicity. Her father, holding Cory, both dozing on the double-wide recliner, looking like a Norman Rockwell painting.

She grabbed her keys quietly, scribbled a note and headed to Wellsville for groceries. And since it happened to be lunchtime, and Trent generally grabbed a sandwich at The Texas Hot, she might just happen to walk by. Stop in.

Totally eighth-grade behavior, and she didn't care a bit. Which made her pathetic or in love, she decided, but the day was warm and breezy, the sun was high, Cory was progressing wonderfully and Alyssa felt positively euphoric.

As she parked the car on a side street, she dialed Trent's number.

"Lyss? That you? How's everything? Is Cory okay?"

His opening line was totally understandable because she never called him. Ever. Naturally he'd jump to worst-case scenario. She drew a breath and waded in before she chickened out. "She's fine. Everything's fine. I was just in town to grab some groceries and I thought…"

"You're in Wellsville?"

"Yes," she replied.

"Where?"

"On Main. Just outside the…"

"Texas Hot," he finished for her. "Turn around."

She did, eyeing the window of the fifties-style restaurant.

"Check the counter."

She did and saw him seated alongside Jeff Brennan, then had to feign surprise.

"And then come in and join us for lunch." He said this last as he approached the door, a broad smile in place.

She opened the door and he met her on the other side, his smile disarming, his gaze assessing the shorts and tank it took her twenty minutes to pick out. He didn't have to know she'd borrowed the shirt from Megan and the cute sandals from her mother. At least the shorts were hers.

"You look wonderful," he murmured.

She shot him a smile, the compliment appreciated. "Thank you…although I'm a bit underdressed considering how you two look."

They'd lost their sport coats, but their shirt-and-tie apparel said young executive all the way.

"I like how you're dressed." Trent said the words lightly but the implication was clear.

Alyssa flushed, then managed a smile when he slipped an arm around her shoulders. "Jeff, think we can find a booth?"

Jeff angled his head toward the back. "Ellie just commandeered one for us. The colonel is leaving."

Trent turned, saluted and waited as an aged marine made his way between the double row of booths, his step unsure, his gaze sharp, his chin held high.

The old man noted Trent. A knowing smile softened his features. "At ease, Captain."

Trent smiled back as the colonel's granddaughter moved ahead of him to open the door. "Enjoy your day, sir."

The colonel's quick glance became an easy look of appraisal as he spied Trent's arm around Alyssa. "Looks like a good day all around, Captain."

Trent squeezed her shoulder, grinning. "One can only hope, sir."

Rolling her eyes, Alyssa shrugged out of his grip and led the way to the freshly wiped booth. She and Trent slid in. Jeff took the seat opposite, pretending discomfort. "Awkward."

"You could leave," Trent suggested.

Alyssa jabbed him. "I can't believe you just said that."

"I can." Jeff raised his coffee cup in salutation and grinned. "But since I'm not going anywhere, the point's moot. You asked me to lunch first. She's the intruder." He added the last with a pointed look in Alyssa's direction.

She jumped in the game, waving toward Trent as Ellie stopped by to freshen their coffees and leave a new one for Alyssa. "You were sitting alongside him when he passed out the invitation, Jeff. Any and all objections should have been stated at that time. End of story."

"Decisive. Adamant. And cute." Jeff winked at Trent. "She might be a keeper."

"I concur." Trent sent a smile of appreciation to Ellie while Alyssa ordered a loaded burger and fries, then turned Alyssa's way, nodding toward the back counter. "They've got graham cracker cream pie, too. Might want to hold off on the fries."

"I can't have both?" she asked good-naturedly.

Arching his brow, he slid his plate toward her. "Share my fries. Eat the pie when it comes. You'll never finish a whole meal and pie."

He was right. She loved that he knew that about her, even after so much time apart.

"Your dad has Cory?"

She smiled. "Yup. Both sleeping. They're pretty copacetic right now, comparing postsurgical scars, hospital stays. Dad keeps lamenting that her pediatric unit had way more fun things to do than his did."

Jeff laughed and leaned forward. "We're all glad she's doing better. You know that don't you?"

Alyssa fought a surge of emotion. People from all over Allegany County had been doing nice things for her, for Cory, for her parents since Cory's illness became known. She didn't realize how many people loved her parents and appreciated their place in the community until the deck was stacked against them, then help came from all directions. "I do. Thanks, Jeff."

He glanced at his watch, sighed and stood. "And while I'd love to play chaperone a little longer, I've got to get back for that California conference call." He scanned the lunch remains before arching a brow toward Trent. "Which means you're buying."

"Like that's a surprise."

Jeff grinned and waved goodbye to Alyssa. "Good seeing you, Alyssa. Glad things are looking up."

She acknowledged that with a nod. "Me, too." She sidled Trent a questioning look before inclining her head to the now-empty opposite bench. "You can move if you'd like."

His grin said too much…or just enough. "I'm fine where I am, thanks. And your burger's heading this way, so I'll just relax and watch you eat."

"What every girl wants. Great."

He laughed and pared down the conversation while she ate, then eyed her pie with longing when Ellie dropped it off.

"You could have gotten your own," she reminded him.

"I'm on a budget."

His words made her remember his pledge for Cory's hospital bill. "Oh, Trent, I—"

"I'm kidding, Lyssa." He pretended a frown and took a guy-sized fork of pie. Luckily the Texas Hot was famous for good-portioned pieces. "Sharing yours means I'm saving you from yourself. I don't want you skipping dinner because you feel guilty about overindulging."

"My hero."

He let one finger slide across the back of her hand, just one broad, thick finger, the pad smooth but firm, the simple press of skin to skin electrifying. "Got a nice ring to it."

"Yes. Well…" She gulped, swallowed, tried not to choke on the pie, then turned his way after sipping water to stave a possible emergency tracheotomy. "Um, actually…" Needing to confess, she paused, glanced away, then brought a slightly guilt-ridden look back to him. "I set this up."

He furrowed his forehead, confused.

"This." She waved a hand around the popular restaurant. "I figured you'd be here, so I came down to town now, hoping we'd meet."

His features relaxed with his smile. He grasped the hand not holding the fork. "I'm glad, Lyss."

"But I probably shouldn't have," she continued.

He brought the hand to his mouth and kissed the skin he'd just caressed. "I disagree."

"Because—"

"Some things aren't worth arguing," he interrupted, his gaze gentle, his touch firm. "There's nothing wrong with this attraction, Lyss. After all, we're both adults."

"Yes, but…"

"And we share a past and a kid."

"That I hid from you." She faced him squarely, needing him to see her flaws, her weakness.

He pondered that for just a moment. "When are you going to tell me the rest, Lyss?"

His direct approach shouldn't have come as a surprise, but it did. "I—"

He squeezed her hand. "Not here. And only when you're ready, okay?"

He'd always sensed things about her. Those foolish insecurities, her shaky self-esteem. Could she just out and out tell him?

Why not?

Gentle words from scripture came back to her, wafting over her like the sunlit streaks of a morning sky. "I will remove their hearts of stone, and plant a new spirit within you."

Her heart had felt like stone for a long time. Too long. Meeting Trent's gaze, feeling the compassion of the kind-hearted townsfolk, knowing they cared for a child not their own…

It felt good. Wondrously good. As if no matter what she'd

done, where she'd been, these people would still offer a hand of mercy. Compassion. Forgiveness and acceptance.

She took a deep breath and nodded. "Soon. Okay?"

His gaze gentled, the look of understanding nearly undoing her right there. He gave her fingers one more light squeeze. "I'll be here."

Three simple words that promised so much. Maybe too much?

He smiled.

And she smiled back, reading his silent message. It wasn't too much, not at all, but just enough. They sat there, gazes locked, goofy grins in place until Ellie cleared her throat with the check.

Trent gave Alyssa's hand one last squeeze, then reached for the slip of paper. "I've got that, Ellie. Thanks."

She grinned, winked at Alyssa and cleared their remaining dishes. "Looks like a good lunch all around. Jeff got out of paying again," she slanted a teasing look to Trent. "And you got the girl."

Trent laughed, stood and extended a hand to help Alyssa out of the seat. "I got the better end of the deal, that's for sure."

"Or I did." Alyssa grinned up at him, amazed at how wonderfully, delightfully normal this all seemed. Was this what she'd been missing all these years? The chance to be ordinary? And who would have thought of everyday regular as being this much fun, this... perfect?

Trent grasped her hand while they waited near the front door to pay the bill.

The constant flow of patrons in and out of the Texas Hot kept the pace frenetic most of the day, including right now, but the organized chaos seemed almost peaceful to Alyssa.

More of Ezekiel's wise words came back, nipping her with simplicity. "They will be my people, and I will be their God."

What had Trent whispered to her in the hospital? Something about walking by faith, not by sight?

Alyssa was a pragmatic person. She'd had to be, but something in that idea, the thought of embracing belief, trusting the unknown, putting her faith in something bigger, stronger and more powerful than she could think of being tempted her.

Could God forgive what she'd done? The choices she'd made in the past, things that snowballed out of her control?

Yes, if she believed scripture. Jesus cleansed the lepers. Sighted the blind. Washed away sin by His hand and His blood.

Trent tugged her closer once the bill was paid, slipped an arm of comfort around her shoulders and pressed a gentle kiss to her hair as he walked her out the door. Little things. Tiny actions that meant so much…felt so good.

Bright sun bathed her face as they stepped onto the sidewalk, its warmth a benediction.

Trent held her hand one last moment, then pressed her fingers, his eyes telegraphing a look of longing as they skimmed her face. Her mouth. He leaned forward, then caught himself and pulled back. "I'll stop by tonight to take Jaden to football practice."

"Thank you."

She meant for more than the promised ride, but his smile said he knew that. Giving in, he leaned forward and swept a quick kiss across her lips, the momentary sensation a whispered promise. "See you later."

"Okay." The touch of his mouth left her breathless. The hinted promise of a future with the man whose past she shared intimately.

She watched him head south on Main, while she turned north toward her car, but neither one made it more than ten paces before turning back to wave one last time.

Trent grinned.

So did Alyssa.

She made a note to call Megan and rethank her for lending her the shirt. Girls had to stick together in matters of the heart and Alyssa had forgotten how nice it was to have a girlfriend around. Not to mention the support system of her parents.

Breathing deep of fresh, clean air, Alyssa climbed into her car, headed for the local supermarket and for the first time in a long time, felt like she was home.

Chapter Twenty-two

Back at her parents' she balanced multiple plastic sacks off her fingers, then grumbled when she couldn't quite manage the back door.

"I've got it." Her father came into view, sent her a look of fake exasperation and pushed open the screen door. "You could have made two trips. Or called me."

"Force of habit. Is Cory up?"

"Mommy, I'm putting my shoes on all by myself! Gwandpa and me are going outside because we're finking about where to put our doghouse."

"Thinking." Alyssa stressed the opening sound, then bent to Cory's level. "Put your tongue between your teeth, like this."

Cory watched Alyssa's mouth, then repeated the action. "Th… thinking. There! I got it, Mommy!"

"You did." Alyssa leaned in and gave her a smacking kiss. "Good job, sugarplum. Now see if you can manage those shoes on your own while I put away groceries, okay? Then I'll join you and Grandpa."

"Did you remember my prescription?" Gary eyed the multiple bags as he emptied one.

"I did. It's still in the car."

"There's more?"

Alyssa laughed at his look. "Just a little. And some of it's for my place, although we end up eating over here half the time anyway."

"But that's okay," her father insisted, his tone reassuring. "Cooking for one is no fun, and because one or two of us is usually working, that just leaves the kids with whoever's left. It makes no sense to cook separately a hundred feet apart."

"Thanks, Dad."

His smile reminded her of the dad he'd been when she was Jaden's age, before puberty and expectations messed everything up. "You're welcome. Come on, kid." He pointed to the back door. "Let's check this out. See what might work."

Cory stood, righted her shirt and grabbed a small notepad and a crayon. "I'll write fings down, okay?"

He met her serious look with one of his own, then tapped the matching notebook in his chest pocket. "Me, too. Then we'll compare notes."

Cory squared her shoulders, satisfied. "Perfect."

Seeing them stroll out the door, intent on their mission and of like minds, Alyssa had another reason to offer thanks, not only for their combined improved health, but for their relationship. Cory's innocent delight balanced Gary's gruff exterior.

Only the gruffness had waned while her father's attitude toward her had gentled. Once she set the groceries away and stowed the bags for recycling, Alyssa grabbed her own notebook and her newfound confidence and tracked down her father and Cory by the swing set her father had installed that week. "How are the doghouse plans coming?"

Cory pumped the two-person glider, grinning with independence. Gary patted his chest pocket. "Got my notes. She's got hers. We're good."

Alyssa reached up and gave him a kiss on the cheek. He looked a little surprised and startled but pleased. Definitely pleased. "You must want something."

She laughed. He used to say things like that to her, teasing her, when she was a kid. She handed over her notebook, not bothering with introductions. "Check this out. See what you think."

He quirked a brow, then opened the notebook, his gaze intent as he scanned the pages. When he got to the page where she'd graphed out space, he turned it sideways for the landscape view, then nodded, thoughtful, withdrew the pencil from his pocket and jotted notes in the margins.

Alyssa stood by, pretending patience, silently drumming up whatever reasonable argument she might need to tip the scales in her favor.

When he finished checking the pages, he went back to the second one, the page filled with facts and figures pertaining to the number of annual weddings in their area, the projected gross versus net profit, staffing requirements and necessary upgrades. Then he cocked a brow to her. "This your idea?"

She nodded, standing firm. "Yes, sir."

"And you don't mind taking time to oversee the project? Hire the contractors, check their work? Take this on?"

Alyssa frowned, not understanding.

Gary waved the hand with the pencil toward Cory. "'Cause I'm kind of busy now. I've got other fish to fry. And while I'm glad to help run the restaurant, a whole new angle like this—" he waved the notebook toward her, a small smile spreading over his face "—needs a manager. Someone who loves the restaurant and catering business and knows how to set up a party, plan a menu, deal with slightly insane women otherwise known as brides and make everything come off smoothly on the front lines." He raised a brow. "You think you can handle all that, Alyssa? Because I wouldn't trust such a big part of the family business to anyone else."

Tears pricked her eyes.

He noticed right off and mock-scowled. "Oh, for pity's sake, don't go gettin' all mushy on me. Restaurant managers don't cry. Ever."

She grabbed him in the first real hug they'd shared in a long, long time. "This one does. You're sure, Dad? You really like the idea?"

He returned the hug and snuffled, then coughed, trying to

cover his own emotions. Alyssa let him think it worked. "I like it a lot. It's a good use of what's become unused space and these days a business can't afford the albatross of wasted space." He sighed. "And I can't deny I haven't thought of doing banquet work downstairs, but the amount of work it entails would have been impossible with Mom and I. Now it's not."

She nodded. "My thoughts exactly. And the way it flows into Mom's garden along the hill is perfect for pictures. And did you see my notes on the last page about hosting holiday parties?"

"Which means I'll have a banquet room to decorate on top of everything else." He pretended annoyance, but Alyssa saw the gleam of anticipation in his eyes.

She grinned. If there was one thing her father did right, it was holiday decorations, from the gorgeous lamp-lit crèche he erected on the knoll near the restaurant's main entrance, visible from both the road and the valley below, to the thousands of lights he strung along posts, around windows, framing shutters and valances with bright Christmas color. "But this year you have Jaden to help."

Her father's smile broadened. "Don't think I haven't thought of that. And by the time he's off to college, I'll have this one working alongside me. Helping her grandpa make things pretty."

Alyssa pressed a little closer. "Dad, I—"

But Gary shushed her with a shake of his head and a frown, refusing to hear her apology. "I should have done better by you, Alyssa."

Alyssa returned his frown and waved her hand toward the house and the restaurant atop the hill beyond. "Better than working hard? Providing me with everything I needed? A home, a job, parents who loved me?"

Gary shrugged that off. "That's a parent's job, isn't it? But I went too far. I kept thinking that if you did great in school, hung with the right people, you'd go far. That maybe you wouldn't have to work every weekend, every holiday, every evening trying to make a living."

"But I love working at The Edge." She turned to face him fully, not understanding. "I always did."

"I wanted more for you."

Alyssa sighed, eyeing Cory. "Isn't that the way of it, Dad? We want so much for our kids we don't see the forest for the trees."

"That's how it was." He stretched an arm out around her and pulled her close, another first. "And I'm sorry."

"Me, too."

"You're not crying, are you? Again?" he asked in exasperation.

"No." She sniffed.

"Good because the building season around here is only so long and if we're going to get approvals and contractors lined up, we need to get a move on."

"Now?"

"Right now," Gary affirmed. "With Walker Electronics on the upswing, people will be a little more willing to part with their cash. I'd just as soon they part with it for us." He smirked, then turned serious again. "I'll talk to the bank about a loan once we have figures. If we swallow the profits of a good opening season to repay the loan, then we're floating clear with profits from that point forward. Which will mean we go into spring a lot more solvent than we have the last five years."

He released her arm and nodded toward the house. "Scout out contractors. Get bids. Have them do up a plan ASAP so we can present it to the town board meeting in July. If all goes well, we can have our approvals, a prototype drawing, and be booking weddings for next year within a couple of weeks."

A couple of weeks. Alyssa couldn't believe how quickly this was all coming together.

She folded the notebook shut and headed for the house. "I'm on it. Oh, and Dad?"

"Yeah?"

He'd put the gruff tone back in his voice, but it was tossed in just for her benefit.

She smiled and held the notebook aloft. "Thanks."

He met her smile with a long-missed look of affection and a shrug. "Get to work, kid." He jerked his head in Cory's direction. "Can't you see I'm busy?"

She laughed and headed across the lawn, laying mental plans with every forward step, feeling like a new world of possibilities had just opened.

The afternoon sun warmed her from without. Her father's vote of confidence did the same from within.

"A new heart within you…"

The sweet words tumbled through her brain once more, the promise of hope, of being washed new and clean.

Lovely. Just lovely.

Chapter Twenty-three

Alyssa saw Trent's number flash in her phone screen on Saturday morning and snatched it up way too fast to be considered subtle. "Hey."

"Hey, yourself." His slow tone hugged an undercurrent of laughter and something else. Something warm and personal, like a walk beneath the stars, hands clasped, shoulders bumping now and again as they scouted out celestial patterns. "Is it okay if I take Jay shopping after practice today? He needs some things for the camp coming up at Baileview and I've got free time."

"It sounds wonderful," Alyssa admitted. "I'm working, though, to cut Mom some slack. Can you guys handle it without me? And do you need money?"

"Like you know the first thing about cleats, mouth guards and athletic supporters." Trent made a pained noise. "No, this is just me and the kid. And I've got it covered, thanks, although I wouldn't say no to a home-cooked meal in exchange sometime. Sometime soon."

The sound of that, of cooking for Trent and the kids, went beyond feeling good to positively giddy. And Alyssa knew her way around a kitchen, even a small one like hers above the garage. "I'm off on Tuesday."

"Tuesday it is." The way he said it, the sure-of-himself tone in his voice, made it sound like a date.

With kids, she reminded herself.

That realization did nothing to curb her anticipation, which was just plain silly because she saw Trent regularly when he dropped Jaden off and picked him up, right?

But this was different and she knew it. What's more, he knew it. "Gotta go. Kids are arriving. This pickup practice stuff has turned into a regular event."

Because of the efforts he and Chris Russo had put in, she knew. Even though it was early summer, football held a big place in the heart of Allegany County. Real gridiron fans considered nothing too much or too early to prepare their teams for fall.

And if all went according to current plan, The Edge's new lower-level facility would be well under way by then. She and Gary had met with two contractors on Friday and had another scheduled for Monday afternoon, a former Wellsville resident whose work came highly recommended by people at the northern end of Allegany County. "You don't mind dropping Jay off for work tonight, right?"

"Do I get to see the boss?"

She flushed and smiled, pretending to misunderstand him. "Most likely. And the boss's daughter." Gary was coming into work for the first time since his surgery, which should lend a welcoming flavor to the evening dinner crowd.

Trent laughed out loud. "Perfect."

She hung up the phone, spent the morning working on ad copy for the local papers and the upcoming full-color wedding guide put out by a consortium of local businesses, then headed to work. All the while feeling like the pieces of her life had come together like a patchwork quilt in Maude McGinnity's quaint shop, her edges custom-matched, not a wrinkle in sight.

One look at her mother's face that night sent her hope-filled day into the Dumpster. "Mom, what is it? What's wrong? Is Cory okay?"

Alyssa moved farther into the kitchen and saw Aunt Gee sitting at her mother's table, the look on her face a mix of sorrow and chagrin. "Alyssa, I'm sorry. I came east to check on your dad and Cory, and…" Her voice caught, wary and uncertain. "I had no idea they didn't know…"

Gee's voice trailed off, her normally bright complexion pale with remorse, her surprise visit an unexpected reality check for Alyssa.

Gary stepped into the room behind Alyssa, his face creased in concern. "Susan, what's up? What's wrong?" Spotting his youngest sister-in-law, he paused, his expression assessing the mood. "Gee? Didn't expect to see you here. What's going on?"

Susan didn't meet his gaze or respond to his questions. She moved across the floor, her gaze trained on Alyssa. "Why didn't you call us? Tell us? Didn't you know we would always come for you? Help you?"

Alyssa shot a look toward Gee, then swallowed hard.

Susan grabbed Alyssa's hands and squeezed. "We would have helped you. We're your parents. We've always been your parents. Didn't you know that?"

Gary's voice took a distinct downhill turn as he read the combination of Alyssa's expression, his wife's voice and his sister-in-law's anxiety. He slipped an arm around Alyssa. "What's wrong? Are you in some kind of trouble?"

She shook her head, blindsided by a past she'd desperately tried to keep buried. "No. I—"

Susan gripped Alyssa's hands with shaky fingers. "I'd have been there in a heartbeat, Alyssa. If only I'd known."

"I knew."

The young male voice from the door drew their collective attention. Jaden stepped in, his lips pale, his face ashen.

Alyssa frowned, ignoring her father's sputter beside her. "What do you mean, Jay?"

Jaden faced her, dead-on. "That he beat you. That you pretended it didn't happen because we had no money and nowhere to go, but I knew all along." He stepped farther into the kitchen, his eyes locked on Alyssa's, their depth a mix of sorrow and accusation. "I used to pray we'd just leave. Go someplace else.

Anyplace else. And then things got better when Cory was born and I hoped it was over, until…"

His voice trailed off, the broken voice of a boy becoming a man, on the cusp of puberty, a boy who knew too much, too soon.

Dear God, no. Please don't let me have been that stupid. That blind. That foolish.

Her father grasped her arm, the touch firm but gentle, and yet enough to set her off with so many buttons being pushed at once. "Let go of me."

He stepped back, hurt.

Susan reached out. "Dad wasn't going to hurt you, Alyssa. We just want to understand what happened." She sent a look of concern toward Jaden.

He stepped back, his look of abject sorrow breaking Alyssa's heart.

Again.

"Honey, I—" Gary stepped forward again, apology lacing his tone.

"No." Alyssa turned toward her father. "There was nothing you could have done. Or you." She swung back toward Susan, feeling like her world had just toppled out of orbit, her star-soaked planets spinning aimlessly, no hope, no direction. "I made the choices all along. I could have chosen to leave. I didn't."

"It's hard to leave a marriage, Alyssa," Gee counseled from her spot on the far side of the table. Her words attempted comfort, but Alyssa had heard the same lame excuses too many times.

Jaden's voice cut deep once more. "Why didn't we come here? With Grandma and Grandpa? Why did you stay there and let him hurt you?"

"He hurt you?"

No. Oh, no.

Trent's voice entered the melee, the soft click of the back screen door announcing his entrance behind her.

"Lyssa…"

She couldn't think quickly enough to chokehold the emotion

running roughshod over her, but Jay's voice came through, loud and clear, just enough to tip her over the edge. "He hit her a lot when he was drinking. Right up until she lost the baby."

Silence descended. Either that or the floor rose up to meet her.

She needed air. Space. Something open and free, the past clawing and cloying, making it hard to breathe.

"Oh, Alyssa." Tears ran unchecked down Susan's cheeks. Her father's look of disappointment dredged up every put-away feeling of long ago, the ones she thought she'd been able to shelve permanently earlier that week.

Obviously not.

Trent looked shell-shocked and angry. Very angry. Jaden looked irreparably sad, right before he turned and dashed out the door, tracks of tears snaking their way down his cheeks, onto his work shirt.

Trent met her gaze, his face teeming with emotion, then he followed Jaden, the slap of the door silencing the frog song of what had been a sweet summer's night.

She read the looks on their faces. The sorrow. The recrimination. But, hey, nothing more than she thought of herself, right?

She longed to leave, to duck out somewhere, anywhere, a place where censure didn't shadow her every move.

"Mommy? What's wrong?" Cory's worried tone thrust the still-life adults into motion.

Susan swiped at her eyes, pretending nonchalance. "Nothing, sugarplum. Why are you out of bed?"

"I was so firsty." Cory's innocent admission reminded them of her recent struggles.

"I'll get you some water, honey. All you have to do is ask." Susan scooped Cory up, crooning sweet words of quiet comfort while she crossed the room to the sink. The sound of running water punctuated the silence, then she ducked her head to Cory's, hummed a lullaby and carried her back off to bed.

Her mother's words laced pain over comfort. Could it have been that easy all along? Ask and ye shall receive? Knock and the door will be opened? Uncomplicated words of grace and faith, a simple question?

Was she that blinded by her stubbornness?

Her father's strong arms wrapped around her, holding her much as her mother had just done to Cory. "I'm sorry, honey. So sorry."

Wait. He was apologizing? For…?

"I made you think you couldn't come home. That I didn't appreciate you the way you were." He held tight, her father's tears wetting her head, her shoulder. "Can you forgive me, Alyssa? Please? And give me another chance?"

Her head spun, confused. She tried to draw back, but he held tight, as if…fearful.

But that was impossible, right? One look at his face assured her it wasn't.

Her big, strong, tough-as-nails father was scared.

"Dad, I—"

He loosened his grip enough to step back and look into her face. "Please don't run away again."

"I—"

"Please." Heart and soul lay plain on his face, his weathered countenance aged by emotion. "I have so much to make up for, but I want to try. I'm just sorry…"

Tears fell again, his jaw quivering, his face wreathed in gut-wrenching emotion.

Concern for his heart condition snapped her back to the present. "Dad, it's all right. Don't get yourself all worked up. I don't want you to get sick. To have another heart attack."

"Me neither." Susan spoke from the living room entry, her pallor grayed with the evening's events. "But your father's right, Alyssa. We wasted too much time and you suffered for it. I'm not sure how to forgive myself for that."

Her parents' combined guilt and anxiety helped lift a portion of hers. Why hadn't she realized how much they cared? That their love outweighed any disapproval she felt? "Maybe we can just start fresh?"

"Oh, baby." Susan moved forward and joined her arms with Gary's, hugging Alyssa. Holding her. "I would be grateful to you and God for that chance. To think what you went through…" She stepped back and held Alyssa's face between her hands, much like Cory liked to do. "We love you, Alyssa. Just the way you are. Always."

The ring of Susan's phone pulled her attention away. She stepped aside, answered, then agreed in a low tone. "That's a good idea. Yes, thank you. We'll see you tomorrow."

Alyssa brought her chin up, ready to face whatever else might come her way. "Jaden?"

"Trent's keeping him tonight. He thought it best." She sent Alyssa a look that combined compassion and sorrow. "I agreed. I hope that's okay. He just seemed—"

"Distraught. Angry. Overwhelmed." Alyssa drew a deep breath. "I had no idea he knew, but that was foolishness on my part. Thinking I could hide things from him. He's a smart boy."

"Who loves his mother," Gary reminded her. He reached an arm around her again and squeezed. "We'll get him through this. And you. And us," he added, a hint of his gruffness added to that last. "Prayer and time, Alyssa. They work wonders."

Remembering the clutch of emotions on her son's face and the anger she glimpsed in Trent's eyes, Alyssa could only pray her father was right.

Chapter Twenty-four

A part of Trent wanted answers. A bigger part wasn't sure what questions to ask.

He'd sat with Jay, comforting his tears, a mix of anger, sadness and frustration, and had to fight the urge to lay hands on someone. With Vaughn Maxwell dead, his choices were severely limited.

That didn't quell the urge, unfortunately.

He prayed once he got Jaden settled for the night. He repeated the litany as day broke over the eastern hills, the glowing sun flooding the valley with bright, sloping light.

What seemed sweet and easy yesterday morning was anything but uncomplicated now. Seeing Jaden's face, hearing his words, Trent recognized the depth of feeling in the boy. His boy. His son.

Anger that Alyssa would let Jaden be exposed to that kind of life steamrolled him.

Sadness that she'd endured the violence of a man's hands made it worse.

And the thought that another innocent child lay dead as a result of a parent's depravity hit below the belt.

Jay wandered out of Trent's bedroom a while later, looking unkempt, dazed, frustrated and confused.

Ditto for Trent.

"Hey." He held out an arm to Jay.

The boy shrugged it off.

Trent weighed his options. Push in? Back off? He went with his gut, remembering how often he'd wished there was someone around to just give him a hug. He wrapped Jay into his arms and held on. "Sorry, man."

Jay snuffled. "Yeah."

Trent hung on tighter. "No, I mean it. I'm really sorry. I'm sorry things got messed up from the beginning with your mom and me. If they hadn't…"

"None of this would have happened."

"Exactly." Trent sighed. "But it did."

"Yup." Jay's voice stayed low, his affect flat.

What could he say to him, this son he was just beginning to know, a kid who'd been through the wringer?

And what could he say to Alyssa, knowing what she and Jay suffered?

Sorry didn't cut it. Not when the list was this long, this convoluted. For the moment all he could do was hold Jay and pray, and it seemed like too little too late.

The look on Jay's face had Trent shelving the idea of church. While the intent would be notable, Jay wasn't ready to face the world after owning what he knew last night. Especially if Lyssa was in the church.

How had this all happened? When had life taken a sharp left turn again?

Not again, an inner voice nudged. *Still*.

Trent squared his shoulders, seeing the truth at last. From one wrong sprang many, each adding weight to a poorly chosen path. Hadn't he made mistakes along the way? His weren't visible, but they existed, as surely as Alyssa's did. Only his indiscretions were hidden. But out of sight didn't make them less wrong.

Trent blew out a breath. He and Jay needed to have a long, frank talk about some very important things. And when the talk was over, Trent would make a pledge to be the very best father he could be, from this point forward.

And then he'd seek out Alyssa with the same mission in mind. He might be powerless to fix the past, but he had the chance to fix himself and that might be a big part of the catalyst they needed.

Alyssa stopped by the practice green on her way to work that afternoon. Trent spotted her at the far end of the field in a copse of trees, watching. Waiting.

Chris had the group involved in a series of drills. Trent used the diversion to jog down and meet her, having no clue what to say or do, but at least he'd had some time to think things through.

Vaughn Maxwell had seemed suspect from the moment Trent pulled up his stats on the Internet, but he'd let it slide. Asked no questions. Now he had no choice but to ask.

He thought he could be tough. Strong. Maybe even a little rigid after hearing Jaden's story the night before, but as he drew closer, those thoughts went out the window because this was Alyssa. Seeing her, drawing closer, feelings replaced logic, and the very idea that anyone would hurt her, lay hands on her, sent his blood boiling again.

Stopping just short of contact, he asked the question that kept him up all night, Jay's short statement that sent Trent's thoughts back to Clay, a little boy lost through no fault of his own. "Tell me about the baby."

Sorrow shaded her features even as growing strength firmed her jaw. "It was a little girl, born in my sixth month. She weighed less than two pounds. She was…" Her hands made motions as if clutching a small doll. Rocking it. The expression of love and loss mirrored his memories of Clay, gone too soon. "Tiny. Skinny. And so absolutely perfect." Tears trickled out of her eyes. She didn't seem to know or care, caught up in the remembered sight of her lost child. "I named her Liliana."

"Pretty."

"Yes." She huffed out a breath, hugged herself and kept her gaze trained beyond Trent for long seconds, then turned. "I hated myself for staying. Things had gotten better after Cory's birth. Vaughn stopped drinking. He was so proud of Cory. He even went to church with us a few times, but then he had another bad year on the ranch. Drought. No help. No money to pay someone to help." She swallowed a lump in her throat. "He violated water rights agreements and got slapped with some heavy fines we couldn't afford. He started drinking again, and I knew what that meant."

She paused, breathing in and out, her face a study of regret. "I didn't tell him about the baby. I hadn't gained much weight and he wasn't around often. I'd made plans to leave while he was on a trip north to sell some gear. I thought I'd timed things just right." She sighed, and lifted one shoulder in a half shrug. "I was wrong. He came home, demanding his rights and discovered I was pregnant."

Trent really, really wanted a piece of this Maxwell guy. He scowled, hating the images her story brought to mind, but wanting her to be open at long last.

She bit her lower lip, her eyes reflecting the emotions of that night. Her desperation. His brutality.

"He didn't need another mouth to feed, only he didn't say it quite that nicely. I miscarried forty-eight hours later, while he was up north, drinking with his buddies, probably toasting his success."

"Alyssa."

She still didn't look at him. "If I'd left sooner, she'd be alive, Trent. I don't know how to forgive myself for that. All this—" she fanned a hand toward the practice field, the town, the community "—was here, waiting for me. If only I'd come back sooner, she might be alive. Toddling around. Sucking her thumb and borrowing Cory's ni-ni. But she'll never have that chance and I don't know how to move beyond these feelings of guilt."

He reached out and pulled her close, needing to hold her, help her, not knowing how, but understanding she needed comfort, not more censure. Knowing Alyssa's self-esteem issues, he was pretty sure she'd raked herself over the coals repeatedly. "Day by day. Step by step. Just like you've been doing, Lyss."

"But…"

"No buts. God promised he would never forsake us. That he wouldn't leave us orphaned, remember?"

"Yes." A soft sigh accompanied the single word, a tiny sound, half hope, half resignation.

"Reverend Hannity brought me a check this morning."

"For?"

"To help cover the cost of Cory's hospital stay. He approached the congregation and they voted unanimously to use ten percent of the building fund to help Cory because your parents and The Edge have been such a big part of Jamison and Wellsville. They wouldn't take no for an answer." He stepped back, tipped her chin up and met her eyes. "You're not alone anymore. 'For if God is with us, then who can be against us?'"

She searched his gaze as if looking for something else, something more, then stepped back, her expression soft but accepting, as if she'd hoped for more but knew better. Her polite smile confirmed it, making him feel like a first-class jerk. She tipped her head toward the car down the street. "I've got to run. I'm working till closing tonight."

"I'll bring Jay home later."

"Thanks, Trent. For everything."

The hint of finality in her parting words dogged his heels, but time constraints worked against him.

He headed back up field, determined to finish practice, then have a heart to heart with his son about what makes a man a man.

And then maybe pay Alyssa a little visit at The Edge.

"Jay? You done with that?" Trent motioned toward Jay's half-eaten plate.

"Yeah."

The lack of affect in Jaden's voice told Trent it was time to have a chat before self-pity established too strong a hold in his son's psyche. He reached out a hand to Jay's arm. "You mad at your mom?"

To his surprise, Jaden shook his head.

"Me?"

"No." Jaden propped his elbows on the table, scowled, nudged the plate of food aside and put his head in his hands. "Me."

Him? Trent pressed forward. "Why would you be mad at yourself, Jay? You've done nothing wrong."

"I didn't stop him."

His words gripped Trent. He stood, circled the corner of the table and stooped, looping an arm around the boy's shoulders. "You were a kid, a little boy. It wasn't your place to stop him."

Jaden shrugged, unable to talk, tears misting his eyes.

"Jay—"

What could he say? What could he do to make this better when he'd tortured himself over Clay's death for years, knowing he could have done nothing, but wishing he had?

A snippet from Colossians came to him, short and succinct, Paul's soothing words a benediction. "For He has rescued us from the dominion of darkness and brought us into the kingdom of the Son He loves."

"Jay, I wish I could change the way things have happened. If I could, I'd go back in time and fix it all, but we don't have that option."

Jay shrugged, defeated.

Trent would have none of that. He angled himself sideways and raised his son's gaze to meet his own. "But our options from this moment forward are limitless and if you and I are the men we want to be, need to be, then I've got a little plan that just might makes things right."

"A plan?" Jay's shoulders straightened slightly. "What kind of plan?"

"The kind that fixes things by bringing people together instead of wrenching them apart." He leaned forward and whispered in Jaden's ear, the boy's improving posture saying he liked what he heard.

"Now?"

"Tonight. Think we can do it?"

Jaden reached up a hand for a high-five. "I know we can, Dad."

Alyssa moved down the curving staircase and surveyed the lower level of the restaurant with a critic's eye. Yesterday this had seemed quite important. So special. Now, in light of Gee's ill-timed pronouncement and Jaden's confession, her new venture didn't seem all that significant.

She eyed the room, the high ceiling, the three-quarter length windows that let light pour in. Conversely, the brightly lit room would gleam against the dark hill at night, a priceless advertisement for a well-run business.

But it meant nothing compared to Jaden's loss of respect. She'd worried about him all day, but took Trent's advice to give him time. Time to think. Regroup. A chance to heal. How sad that by doing what seemed noble at the time, she'd made the worst choice possible. And now Jaden would pay for her mistakes. Again.

A movement caught her eye. She crossed to the far glass door and stepped out, scanning the hill.

Nothing.

Frowning, she turned to go back inside, ready to shut things down. They closed early on Sunday nights, and Alyssa was more than ready to call it a day.

A small sound paused her. She stopped, held her breath and looked around. A deer maybe? Perhaps a lost fawn? Evening shadows deepened the shade along the hill's western edge, the most likely place for a young animal to hover, picking its way.

Still nothing.

Obviously her nerves were shot. Understandable. Then, as she crossed the short expanse of grass to the door, music wafted her way from somewhere inside. Strains of Garth Brooks filled the air as he mulled the choices he'd had, the ones he'd made and how he thanked God for prayers that remained unanswered.

Was it coincidence that someone was playing that song on the old jukebox?

Or was it…

"Alyssa."

Trent.

She turned, a part of her longing to see him. A more timid part wished she could run and hide, but she'd promised herself that would never happen again. She tucked that part away and faced her first love, her only love. And their son.

He approached her from the far corner, Jaden alongside, the boy's face showing traces of maturity that hadn't been as notice-able yesterday. That stung.

Palms sweating, Alyssa swiped her hands against the sides of her pants. "Hey, guys."

She watched them draw close, not knowing what to expect, her heart beating a quick rhythm in her chest, making her glad the jersey top was loose-fit. She drew a deep breath as they came alongside, then turned toward her son. "I owe you an apology."

He stood still, watching her, his eyes not haunted like they were last night but still shadowed by events he couldn't control. Right then she made a silent vow to do whatever it took to van-quish those shadows. "I made mistakes, Jay. Big ones. And then I fooled myself into thinking they wouldn't affect you. I was wrong and I'm so sorry. Can you forgive me?"

He threw himself into her arms, his hug telling her the little boy still lingered within the maturing young man. Tears stung her eyes, but she blinked them back, held him, tousled his head of curls because she knew he hated it and then looked up when Trent cleared his throat.

She sent him a watery smile of thanks.

He rolled his eyes and handed over a wad of tissues from a side pocket.

"Uh, Jay?"

"Oh, yeah. Right." Jaden stepped back, swiped a sleeve across his eyes and faced his mother, his expression serious. "We came over because we needed to talk to you."

Uh-oh.

She'd promised herself she'd be stoic. Strong. Understanding. She'd spent half the day realizing that Jaden would most likely prefer to live with Trent under the circumstances, and despite what that did to her heart, she wanted what was best for him. She braced her feet, straightened her shoulders and lifted her chin. "Of course."

Trent took over. "Lyss, the three of us have a lot of water under the bridge."

True enough. "Yes." She nodded.

"And I think we're all in agreement that we need to move forward. Put the past behind us and begin anew."

She kept her chin firm and met his gaze, but it was a struggle when he looked so amazingly, marvelously wonderful. Those gray-green eyes, so gentle and kind. Imploring. No, she couldn't deny him this chance with their son, even though the very thought of Jaden living elsewhere wrenched her heart.

But it was his heart she needed to put first. "Go on."

"Well." Trent gave Jaden a shoulder nudge that seemed strangely easygoing for such a difficult conversation. Shouldn't he be more sensitive while wresting her child from her?

Eyes narrowed she glanced from Jaden to Trent and back again, then she heard a sound from above, the tiny sound of a child's laughter. A quick sweep of the hilltop restaurant entrance revealed nothing.

"So, um, Mom…" Jaden cleared his throat, his voice cracked and he sent a look of chagrin heavenward. "We were wondering…"

"Hoping, actually," Trent cut in.

"Really hoping," Jaden added.

"Oh my goodness, cut to the chase, will you?"

Trent grinned at Jaden.

He smiled back at his father.

Trent dropped down to one knee and grasped Alyssa's left hand. "That you would marry us. Me. Well, kind of us because we're a package."

"Trent…"

"Here's the deal." He cut her off smoothly, determined to have his say. "I've loved you for over a dozen years. I lost you once. I don't want to risk losing you again. We belong together." He jerked his head in Jaden's direction. "I asked the kid and he's all for it. Now it's up to you." He stopped talking for long seconds and just met her gaze, his thumb making lazy circles on the back of her hand, the tenderness of the moment doing crazy, wonderful, marvelous things to her heart. "Will you do me the honor of becoming my wife, Alyssa?"

Jaden watched her, eyes wide, his expression hopeful. From above she heard a distinctly familiar giggle again.

Aha. Reinforcements.

She bent and touched her lips to Trent's, feeling the anxiety he hid so well. His nerves delighted her, knowing that coming here and doing this wasn't as easy as he pretended, which made perfect sense because they'd spent a dozen years messing things up. Now they'd have a lifetime to put them right again. She rested her forehead against his, relishing the moment, a dream come true, the second chance she hadn't though she deserved. "I love you, Trent. Yes, I'll marry you. We'll marry you. A package deal."

Jaden fist-pumped the air.

Cheers erupted from the hilltop, a clamor of excited voices heading their way.

"Mommy! Mommy! We're going to get mawwied!!!" Cory raced down the hill looking so much better, her tiny body a bundle of raw, healthy energy.

Alyssa scooped her up. "So it would seem, sugarplum. Would you like to be a flower girl and wear a really pretty dress?"

Cory clasped Alyssa's cheeks between her two hands and squished. "I would wuv to do that, Mommy! And we can twirl and dance and watch the stars come out, like you used to do when I was a wittle girl." She held her arms out to Trent, imploring him to take her, so he did.

Alyssa hugged Jaden, then scanned his face. He met her gaze, then hugged her back. "I love you, Mom."

Four simple words. Music to her ears. "I love you, too."

"So…"

Gary's voice interrupted their little party. Alyssa turned and sought his face in the shadowed light. "Hey, Dad."

"It seems we have a wedding to plan."

Trent nodded. "With your permission, sir."

Gary tipped his head toward the lower level of the restaurant. "I know the perfect place to host the reception."

Alyssa smiled up at him. "Think we can do it in time?"

Gary met her smile with a wink. "We can do anything we want. We own the place. Will that put too much stress on you, though?" He leaned in, his concern genuine. "Planning a wedding and retrofitting this at the same time?"

Alyssa slipped an arm around Trent's waist, then Jaden's. "With all this help? Piece of cake."

"And me." Gee stepped forward with Susan, her expression a mix of happy and worried, the family circle turning a quiet proposal into something more akin to a circus act, but Alyssa wouldn't have it any other way. She'd spent way too much time off on her own. This was home. Family. Forever. "If you still love me, that is."

Alyssa gave Trent's waist a squeeze, a quiet sign that meant they might get to more of the kissing stuff later, once they got rid of pesky family. He laughed and dipped his chin to her hair, the action telling her he got the message and was in full agreement.

"Oh, I love you all right," she told Gee. "And I'm glad you decided to come east. Weddings are big doings and I'm going to need a kitchen coordinator." She angled her head toward her aunt. "Someone that can handle Rocco's moods, Dad's semi-retirement and make sure these weddings come off without a hitch. You up for a job, Gee?"

"Are you serious?"

"Totally. We'll sit down tomorrow and figure up the work

schedule once we decide on contractor, but my goal is to have this facility up and running in a couple of months."

"Just in time to walk down the aisle." Trent caught her eye over Cory's head. "I'm not big on long engagements, Lyss. How about you?"

"Whither thou goest, I will go. Whither thou lodgest, I will lodge." She quoted the sweet verse from Ruth and smiled. "The shorter the better as far as I'm concerned."

"Do we get to wiv in Twent's big new house?" Cory swung about, excitement rosying her cheeks, the high pitch of her voice reminding them all that little girls should be in bed by now.

Trent cuddled her close. "Yes. And you and I can make your bedroom very special and very pretty, okay? Maybe with princesses? And flowers?"

She clapped her hands in glee. "I wuv princesses this much!" She spread her hands wide, delighted.

"But you have to promise me something."

"What?" Round-eyed she met his gaze as though willing to promise the world to get a special, pretty bedroom.

"If you ever get a little sister, you need to share your room with her, okay?"

Cory slapped her two hands to her mouth, the thought of a little sister just too over-the-top to be comprehended. "Oh, I will, Twent! I weally will! And I'll let her play wif all my toys but not my ni-ni, okay? She has to get her own ni-ni."

Trent nodded and bumped heads with her. "Deal." He smiled at Alyssa. "You in, Mom?"

She grinned. "Totally."

Susan commandeered Cory and started heading uphill.

Jaden shuffled back a step. "Um, wait a minute, guys." He copped a pained look that encompassed Trent and his mother. "Does that mean if we ever," he made quotes marks with two fingers from each hand, "'happen' to have a boy, he shares my room? I'm not saying it's a deal breaker, but it bears some serious thought and possible contract renegotiation."

Alyssa laughed, the look on his face priceless.

Trent reached out a fist and noogied his head. "Naw. Preteen boys shouldn't have to deal with spit-up and poopy diapers in their bedrooms. Not when they're tied up night and day with schoolwork and running drills. First things first, after all."

"Oh. Well, then." Jaden nodded acquiescence. "I'm in."

The family began moving uphill. Trent caught Alyssa's hand, holding her back just long enough for one more kiss, a hint of yesterday filled with the promise of tomorrow.

Epilogue

"Honey, are you ready?"

"Yes. Kind of. Almost."

Trent rolled his eyes, assumed an exaggerated look of patience and tapped his watch. "If we're going to get to the cemetery on time, we need to get a move on."

"News flash, soldier. I don't get a move on nearly as fast as I used to. Something about six months of baby on board slows a girl down."

"In some ways." Trent's smile made her blush.

"Are the kids in the car?"

"You mean—" he paused, dramatic, stretching out the words as if pained "—the minivan?"

"That would be the one." She sneaked a peek over his shoulder, saw that Jaden was occupied with his game system and Cory was busily coloring yet another picture for the baby. "Have I mentioned how much I love a guy in uniform?" Taking her time, she gave her husband a thorough kiss that made them just a little later than they were.

But not late enough to miss the Memorial Day services.

He held her close, then backed away, laid his hand atop his tiny son or daughter, and felt the gift of life stirring beneath his fingers. "My entire life has become a miracle. You know that, don't you, Lyss?"

She leaned up and pressed another kiss to his cheek. "Mine, too. You have the flowers?"

"In the van."

"Then let's go."

He pulled into the hillside cemetery a few minutes later and parked along the graveled lane like everyone else. Then they all walked to a small knoll beneath an ancient oak, the glossed, deep green leaves glinting points of light back to the sun, the polished barrels of the honor guard rifles a symbol of strength and honor.

Small flags and wreaths dotted the cemetery, while deep red geraniums splashed color against bright green grass.

Trent held Cory with one arm and Alyssa's hand with the other as the VFW honor guard performed its traditional Memorial Day ceremony, a beautiful and fitting tribute to the fallen.

And when it was done, with the cemetery mostly cleared, they walked uphill to another grave. It was small, almost inconspicuous except for the bright new stone set into the grass.

Clay's name was inscribed on one side. Liliana's on the other. As they knelt to plant the bright array of flowers along the base of the stone, Trent realized that visiting his baby brother's grave didn't hurt quite so much as it used to.

"Mommy, are they in heaven?"

The flowers planted, Alyssa nodded, a tear crawling its way down her cheek, one arm around Cory while the other was slipped around Jaden's waist. "Yes, honey."

"Will I see them someday?"

Her sweet innocence brought a smile through the tears. "Yes. God wouldn't have it any other way, sugarplum."

Cory contemplated that a moment, her expression thoughtful. "When baby Clay or Mandy gets born, I'm going to let them share my blanket after all."

Jaden stooped down. "Hey, kid, that's nice of you."

"Well, I'm four now." Like that made all the difference.

Trent smiled and laid his cheek against Alyssa's hair. "True. You're getting big."

"And Miss Megan was telling me in Sunday school that it's really good to share."

"She's right," Alyssa agreed.

"So I think I'll share my blanket with the baby. Most of the time."

Seeing Jaden's grin, Trent noogied his son's head, remembering last Memorial Day. He'd stood here—aside and apart, most people not yet knowing who he was—and prayed for the families of the fallen. And for Clay.

One simple year had made a world of difference. He slipped an arm around Alyssa's shoulders and stepped back. "Hey, guys, Grammy's waiting and she's got food."

Jaden picked up Cory and headed for the car. "I'll get her buckled in."

Alyssa paused at the edge of the knoll, turned back and blew a kiss in the air. Trent planted a very real one to her temple. "I'm glad we put her ashes here, Lyss."

She reached up, kissed him and smiled, his heart stuttering all over again. The smile that won the boy's heart so long ago held the man's heart captive now. "Me, too. It's important to have family together."

He hugged her shoulders, peace settling in alongside the old pain, joy overtaking the nooks and crannies of his heart, his soul.

For the first time in nearly three decades, Trent Michaels had his very own family. And it felt good.

* * * * *

Dear Reader,

I first saw Allegany County while watching a friend's son play in the Little League state championship in Wellsville. It was love at first sight. The rolling hills, the worn infrastructure, the hopeful people all spoke of an area that refused to be kept down by economic pressures. I knew I had to set books here.

Kids make mistakes. As a mother of six I found teenage affairs of the heart were nothing to be taken lightly, and having married my high school sweetheart, I felt I understood those growing pangs. But sometimes a combination of events thrusts people onto unexpected paths. I wanted a story of sacrifice and first love, of mistakes and missteps. I've encountered my share of surprises throughout my life. In all cases, good and bad, God was there, ever-present, omniscient, helping, guiding.

But what if you didn't believe that? What if your mistakes were compounded and you couldn't see the forest for the trees? This is how I see Alyssa Langley, a young woman whose life course was altered by a series of choices that left a twisted, turning trail, a path so wound upon itself that it took tragedy to iron it out. Then add in Trent Michaels, a boy tossed away by his parents as if he was yesterday's trash. His longing is exacerbated by Alyssa's deception. Their story is the first I've set in Allegany County, one of God's prettiest places on the planet. It's a story of second chances, a tale of new light chasing old shadows. If you like this story, or just want to chat with me, visit me at ruthloganherne.com, e-mail me at ruthy@ruthloganherne.com, find me on Facebook or Goodreads.com, or you can snail mail me c/o Steeple Hill Books, 233 Broadway, New York, NY 10279.

And until we meet again, may God hold you in the palm of His hand.

Ruthy Logan Herne

1. Spurred by "age" and "stage," young people often make mistakes. Do you have things from your youthful past that you've regretted? How did you move on? Make amends?

2. Alyssa's personality is part nature, part nurture. How did her relationship with her father negatively affect her life and influence her choices?

3. Trent was abandoned as a boy, a heartless act by callous parents. How did that affect his later reaction when he discovered he had unknowingly been a parent for eleven years?

4. Cat Morrow has a simple place in this book, as a "been there, done that" person who strives to improve her lot in life by working hard and embracing faith and morality. Do we have "bit players" in our lives, people whose quiet contribution helps us to stay on course?

5. I love putting precocious children in books. Grown-ups can glean so much from the innocence of a child. How does Cory's Pollyanna nature break through Trent's walls of anger?

6. Reverend Hannity is a good guy. You sense that. Feel it. And yet he has a past that went untold until his daughter arrived in town as an adult. Her subsequent marriage and presence provides him with a family he never knew he had, just when he and his wife were facing their elder years alone. Do mistakes of the past sometimes become the hope of the future?

7. Alyssa's shame because of her teenage choices became her crutch later on. Embarrassed by what she'd done once she

moved out west, she didn't want her parents to see her as a chronic failure and stayed too long in a dangerous relationship. How often does self-guilt push our choices beyond safe and normal? How can we recognize that and defuse it?

8. Trent appears stellar to the Jamison onlooker, but he alone knows he hasn't always been a paragon of virtue. The difference is he caught himself and reversed his negative behaviors. How does this make him more sympathetic to Alyssa's internal angst and guilt?

9. When Trent realizes Alyssa had been abused, he's angry for two reasons: one, that she subjected a gentle boy like Jaden to that environment, and two, that he didn't press further when he read Vaughn Maxwell's death notice and the bad debt records concerning Vaughn's Montana ranch. He'd wondered at the kind of man Vaughn was, but neglected to investigate further. How often does the Holy Spirit nudge us in a direction, only to have us shrug Him off? Pursue our own course?

10. Gary wanted what most parents do: a chance for his daughter to better herself. He didn't see that what she wanted was what he'd already provided, a chance to help run the family business, a business she knew, loved and understood. Why do parents often blind themselves to reality in hopes of thrusting their children to greater heights?

11. Susan is obviously a lovely lady, but she's quietly taken Gary's side all these years, assuming Alyssa was all right in spite of their estrangement. Was her action good or bad? Should she have stood up for Alyssa earlier? Would it have helped? Would it have threatened their marriage?

12. Gary's epiphany comes as a result of Cory's illness and Alyssa's knack for taking over the restaurant. He sees his

choices and guilt clearly. God seems to bring natural forces together on a regular basis to teach us lessons. Will Gary's confession and apology be enough to thrust this family forward?

13. When Susan finds out that Alyssa was in an abusive relationship, she's shocked, hurt and appalled that her daughter was hurt and that Alyssa didn't realize she could always come home, that her parents loved her and cherished her despite their differences, but they'd had little more than incidental contact for years. How do years of apathy erode a person's confidence, his/her self-worth, and those internal feelings of being loved when those feelings are rarely stoked?

14. Trent's original goal was to help the people of Jamison and Allegany County by providing more jobs, more income to a down-trodden community. His goal then widens to include Jaden's well-being, and eventually that of Alyssa, Cory and their unborn child? How did his gift of altruism become a gift to him?

15. Trent's walk to be an achiever, a model child and then a model citizen is pushed along by his need to prove himself valuable, his internal feelings of unworthiness exacerbated by his parents' abandonment, Clay's death and being a notable foster child throughout his formative years. All he ever wanted was a normal family. How did his internal need push him to the story's ending, a chance to feel better about himself in the end and erase his guilt over Clay's death?

INSPIRATIONAL

Inspirational romances to warm your heart & soul.

TITLES AVAILABLE NEXT MONTH

Available April 26, 2011

AN UNLIKELY MATCH
Chatam House
Arlene James

MIRIAM'S HEART
Hannah's Daughters
Emma Miller

HOME TO STAY
Annie Jones

BIG SKY REUNION
Charlotte Carter

THE FOREST RANGER'S PROMISE
Leigh Bale

INSTANT DADDY
Carol Voss

REQUEST YOUR FREE BOOKS!

2 FREE INSPIRATIONAL NOVELS
PLUS 2
FREE
MYSTERY GIFTS

Love Inspired®

Amish widow Hannah Goodloe's son has run away,
and to find him, she needs help—which circus owner
Levi Harmon can provide. If Hannah can convince him.
Read on for a sneak preview of HANNAH'S JOURNEY
by Anna Schmidt, the first book in the
AMISH BRIDES OF CELERY FIELDS *series.*

"I HAVE REASON TO BELIEVE that my son is on your train,"
Hannah said. "I have come here to ask that you stop that
train until Caleb can be found."

"Mrs. Goodloe, I am sympathetic to your situation, but
surely you can understand that I cannot disrupt an entire
schedule because you think your son…"

"He is on that train, sir," she repeated. She produced
a lined piece of paper from the pocket of her apron and
handed it to him. In a large childish script, the note read:

*Ma, Don't worry. I'm fine and I know this is all a part
of God's plan the way you always said. I'll write once I
get settled and I'll send you half my wages by way of general delivery. Please don't cry, okay? It's all going to be all
right. Love, Caleb*

"There's not one word here that indicates…"

"He plans to send me part of his wages, Mr. Harmon.
That means he plans to get a job. When we were on the
circus grounds yesterday, I took note of a posted advertisement for a stable worker. My son has been around horses
his entire life."

"And on that slimmest of evidence, you have assumed that
your son is on the circus train that left town last night?"

She nodded. She waited.

"Mrs. Goodloe, please be reasonable. I have a business
to run, several hundred employees who depend upon me,

not to mention the hundreds of customers waiting along the way because they have purchased tickets for a performance tonight or tomorrow or the following day."

She said nothing but kept her eyes focused squarely on him.

"I am leaving at seven this evening for my home and summer headquarters in Wisconsin. Tomorrow, I will meet up with the circus train and make the remainder of the journey with them. If your boy is on that train, I will find him."

"Thank you," she said. "You are a good man, Mr. Harmon."

"There's one thing more, Mrs. Goodloe."

Anything, her eyes exclaimed.

"I expect you to come with me."

Don't miss HANNAH'S JOURNEY by Anna Schmidt, available May 2011 from Love Inspired Historical.

X

Love Inspired **HISTORICAL**

Save $1.00 when you purchase
2 or more Love Inspired® Historical books.

SAVE
$1.⁰⁰

**when you purchase 2 or more
Love Inspired® Historical books.**

52609783

5 65373 00076 2   (8100)0 11736